TOURIST TRAP

"I'm stuffed!" Nancy announced as she and the Hardys left the restaurant. "I think that was the most delicious meal I've ever had."

Frank nodded in agreement as he linked arms with Nancy, while Joe took her other arm. "We'll walk you back to the hotel," Frank insisted.

Light snow was falling as they made their way down the narrow, winding streets. "I love being in a city where you can walk almost everywhere," Nancy said.

She jumped as headlights suddenly flared behind them and a powerful engine was gunned. Nancy glanced back and saw a car speeding down the center of the street.

As Nancy froze, momentarily blinded, she heard Frank yell, "Look out! He's going to hit us!"

Nancy Drew & Hardy Boys SuperMysteries

DOUBLE CROSSING
A CRIME FOR CHRISTMAS
SHOCK WAVES
DANGEROUS GAMES
THE LAST RESORT
THE PARIS CONNECTION
BURIED IN TIME
MYSTERY TRAIN
BEST OF ENEMIES
HIGH SURVIVAL
NEW YEAR'S EVIL

Available from ARCHWAY Paperbacks

NEW YEAR'S EVIL

Carolyn Keene

AN ARCHWAY PAPERBACK
Published by POCKET BOOKS
New York London Toronto Sydney Tokyo Singapore

This book is a work of fiction. Names, characters, places and incidents are either the product of the author's imagination or are used fictitiously. Any resemblance to actual events or locales or persons, living or dead, is entirely coincidental.

AN ARCHWAY PAPERBACK *Original*

An Archway Paperback published by
POCKET BOOKS, a division of Simon & Schuster Inc.
1230 Avenue of the Americas, New York, NY 10020

Produced by Mega-Books of New York, Inc.

ISBN: 0-671-67467-6

First Archway Paperback printing November 1991

10 9 8 7 6 5 4 3 2 1

Cover art by Frank Morris

Printed in the U.S.A.

IL 6+

NEW YEAR'S EVIL

Chapter One

"I THINK QUEBEC must be the most romantic city on earth," said Bess Marvin, her blue eyes wide with excitement. "I can't believe we're going to spend New Year's Eve here *and* get to watch a movie being made."

"I thought Christmas was over two days ago," said Nancy Drew, "but coming here is the best present of all."

Both girls had dressed in jeans and heavy sweaters under their parkas, but an icy breeze still chilled them. Nancy tugged her blue beret farther down over her reddish blond hair and moved her long, slender legs to keep them warm. Bess was completely bundled up in a violet parka and pink scarf, hat, and mittens. Only her blue eyes and red nose were visible beneath a fringe of blond hair.

"It's so great to get to see Emily, too," said Bess. She waved to a tall, slender woman with large brown eyes, who was talking to one of the camera crews. "I'm glad she thought to call us when they started having all those accidents on the set."

Nancy nodded. "You guys were so busy catching up on each other's lives that we still don't know what's really going on," she teased, pulling the collar of her red down jacket tighter around her neck.

Nancy and Bess had flown to Quebec, Canada, that morning after Bess's second cousin, Emily Anderson, had called. Emily had started working in television a few years earlier. Now she was the production coordinator for *Dangerous Loves,* a Canadian/American television movie about a young French Canadian woman who falls in love with a champion race car driver.

All Nancy knew so far about the trouble on the set was that the filming was behind schedule and way over budget because of a series of setbacks—wrong costumes being delivered, camera dollies that suddenly didn't work, lights falling and breaking. The accidents weren't serious, but there had been enough of them that Emily had become suspicious.

"Just look at that view!" Bess exclaimed, gesturing up and over Nancy's shoulder with a mittened hand.

Nancy glanced back from the bank of the frozen river where she and Bess were standing. Behind them a steep slope led up to the stone walls that encircled Quebec's old Upper Town. Quebec had first been colonized in the 1600s, and the Upper and Lower towns resembled drawings of medieval towns.

"The city is gorgeous," Nancy agreed, wishing she could share it with her boyfriend, Ned Nickerson. "But right now I'm more interested in what's going on down here, on the set." She gestured to the dozen or so recreational vehicles that served as dressing rooms, offices, and equipment rooms for the movie company.

"What do you suppose they're doing now?" Bess asked.

Fifty yards away, out on the frozen surface of the river, members of the film crew were placing bright orange traffic markers.

Emily broke off from talking with one of the crew members and started toward Bess and Nancy. She was wearing a black hooded parka with *Dangerous Loves* embroidered across the back in red and white. Her name was stitched across the front.

"Brr!" Emily said, tightening the drawstring on her hood. "I can't stand this cold. I still haven't gotten used to it."

"I'm too excited to be cold," Bess said. "What's happening out there now?"

"We're setting up for an ice-racing scene," Emily explained. "The movie takes place during Quebec's Winter Carnival, and ice racing is one of the Carnival's big events."

"Ice racing?" Nancy repeated. "You mean, with cars?"

Emily nodded. "I know, it sounds a little strange, but it's really exciting to watch. I saw a test run yesterday, right here on the Saint Charles River."

"Saint Charles?" Bess echoed, sounding puzzled. "I thought the river in Quebec was called the Saint Lawrence."

"That's what I thought, too," Emily said, laughing. "But the Saint Lawrence is over there to the right. The icebreakers keep it open most of the winter, so you can't drive a car on it. This is the Saint Charles. It's a lot smaller."

"Is the ice really thick enough to support cars?" Bess asked, dubiously staring out at the river.

A worried look crossed Emily's face. "I hope so. Our local experts say there are only a few spots we have to avoid."

Nancy pointed to a nearby sign marked Danger. "You mean, like that one?"

Emily nodded. "Uh-huh. Somebody told me that there's a spring under that patch of ice, so it doesn't freeze as quickly. You see how it's a lighter color, sort of bluish? But out in the middle, where they're marking off the race course, there shouldn't be any problems."

"I hope not," Bess said. "You've already had more than your share of accidents on this film."

"We sure have," said Emily. "I'm counting on you and Nancy to find out why, and stop them."

Nancy was about to ask a few questions, but just then someone shouted for Emily.

"Oops, that's David Politano, the director," Emily said. "I'd better run. David's a very talented guy, but he's got a temper you wouldn't believe. I didn't tell him the reason I wanted you guys on the set, by the way. He did agree to let me ask you up, but he didn't much like the idea. Stay out of his way if you can."

"We will," Bess promised.

Emily walked carefully across the ice toward a group of people. At the center of the group was a short, stocky man in his forties whom Nancy assumed was David Politano. His black hair was pulled back into a small ponytail, and a long, bright red scarf was wrapped around his neck. Nancy was too far away to hear what the director was saying, but he was obviously giving a series of orders.

Finally, he clapped his hands once and shouted, "Places!"

A young woman lifted a bullhorn to her mouth and repeated, "Places, please!"

"Look, there's Dennis Conners," Bess whispered, tugging excitedly on Nancy's arm. "He's the male lead. Isn't he luscious? I saw him on TV in 'Thunderstruck,' but he's even more gorgeous in real life."

Nancy found herself agreeing with Bess—Dennis Conners *was* luscious. He was fairly tall, with broad shoulders and a muscular build. His black hair and black eyebrows made a striking contrast to his pale skin and startling blue eyes. He was wearing a white coverall and a thick down parka.

Nancy heard a click and a whir behind her. Glancing back, she recognized tall, lanky Jack Parmenter, Emily's boyfriend. He was the still photographer for the film crew. His job was to take pictures that could be used later for publicity.

He lowered his camera and raked a hand through his spiky blond hair as he surveyed the scene. He gave Nancy and Bess a wink. Then he followed Dennis out onto the ice, snapping pictures as he went.

"Wow," said Bess. "Check out that car!"

A bright red race car was being wheeled into position, about thirty feet from where Nancy and Bess were standing. All the window glass had been removed, Nancy saw, and a row of steel bars installed in place of the windshield.

Dennis, standing by the driver's side of the car, put on a crash helmet. Then he grabbed the upper edge of the door and did a feet-first jump through the window opening.

"Why did he do that?" Bess wondered aloud.

A man standing a few feet from them overheard. "The doors are welded shut," he explained. "For safety."

Bess frowned. "Doesn't that make it hard to get out, if anything goes wrong?"

Thc man shrugged. "They figure the driver is usually better off inside the car. He wears a lot of protective gear, you know."

"Silence, please," the bullhorn sounded. "Silence on the set!"

Emily rejoined Nancy and Bess as a young man stepped forward with a clapper board and said, "*Dangerous Loves,* scene thirty-eight, take one. And . . . *action!*"

Dennis pulled himself out of the car until he

was sitting in the window. He unbuckled his helmet and took it off, triumph written all over his face. Then he looked to the left, and his expression changed to one of anger.

While one of the cameras caught Dennis's expression in a close-up, another camera dollied in toward the front of the race car. Nancy looked where the camera was pointed. A lovely young woman was standing close to another driver. Her light brown hair fluffed out around her face like a halo. Her hand was on his arm.

"That's Marguerite Laforet," Emily whispered to Nancy and Bess. "She plays the female lead, a French Canadian lawyer. The guy she's talking to plays her ex-boyfriend in the movie. He and Dennis are racing rivals."

Just then Nancy was distracted by the roar of a souped-up engine. She turned in time to see a purple-and-gold race car round one of the many bends in the river. It sped straight for the film crew.

"Uh-oh," Emily said, frowning. "That's not in the script. Who is that idiot? He's going to ruin the scene."

"Cut!" Politano yelled. "Whose car is that? Get him off my set!"

The approaching car began to slide sideways across the ice, right toward Dennis's car. The actors and crew members scattered. Only Jack stood his ground and snapped one shot after another.

Just when it seemed that nothing could prevent a terrible crash, the car spun around twice and came to a stop, only a few feet from Dennis's car. A moment later the driver, a man with shaggy brown hair, a square face, and a nose that looked as if it had been broken more than once, climbed out. He gave the shaken crowd a smug smile.

"Good morning, everyone," he said, in a thick French Canadian accent. "I have come to see you work and let you profit of my expert counsels."

"Now, listen to me, Junot," Politano shouted angrily.

"This looks like trouble," Emily murmured. "I'd better get over there."

Nancy pulled Bess onto the ice behind Emily. "Come on, we don't want to miss anything important."

"Good morning, Monsieur Politano," Junot said, with a taunting grin.

"Junot, I told you yesterday, no deal," Politano said loudly. "I don't care if you *are* the ice-racing champion of Quebec. You can do stunt driving for us, as we agreed. But we don't need another technical advisor. We have an excellent one already, François Volnay."

Junot gave a loud sniff. "Volnay?" he said. "A good driver once, before his accident. Now he is good for nothing."

"I understand why they call you Snake, André." Someone in a deep voice had spoken. A tall, thin man of about thirty limped forward. "You hide in the grass, like a snake," the man continued. "Then, when you are sure it is safe, you strike."

"Remember who you are, old man, and who I am," Junot replied with a sneer. "And remember, too, that when these Yankees finish their work and leave Quebec, Volnay, you will again be nothing, but I will still be the champion."

"We shall see," François Volnay said, but Nancy noticed that his face had reddened. He turned and limped back to the riverbank.

"Now, listen here—" Nancy heard Politano begin to tell Junot. Her attention was distracted, however, as another car, a sleek-looking sedan, drew near on the ice. The driver carefully skirted the orange markers and came to a stop a dozen feet from the crowd. All four doors opened. A man with a gray mustache, wearing a fur cap, got out of the passenger seat. Another man, in a leather jacket and beret, climbed out from behind the wheel.

From the backseat two teenage guys got out and studied their surroundings with interest.

Nancy stared at them, looked away, and then snapped her head back as she realized who they were.

"Nancy, look!" Bess exclaimed. "Isn't that Frank and Joe Hardy? What are *they* doing in Quebec?"

There was no mistaking handsome Frank Hardy's six-foot-one frame, dark hair and dark eyes, or the slightly shorter, more muscular build of his blond, blue-eyed brother, Joe.

"And in a car in the middle of the Saint Charles River," Nancy added with a smile.

The Hardys were walking with the two older men, but they stopped when they spotted Nancy and Bess.

A grin lit up Joe's face as he and Frank hurried over. "Hey, what are you doing here?" he asked, as the boys gave Nancy and Bess big hugs.

"We were just wondering that about you," said Bess.

"We came up this morning to get a behind-the-scenes look at ice racing," Frank explained.

Nancy felt the familiar thrill as he bent to kiss her cheek. She knew nothing would ever happen between them because she had Ned, and Frank had a girlfriend, Callie Shaw.

"Henri Dussault, the man in the fur hat," Frank went on, "is an old friend of our dad's.

He invited us to stay with him for a week of R and R. Dussault Motors, his company, sponsors the ice race during Winter Carnival, in February."

"The guy with him is Pierre Desmoulins," Joe added. "He's coordinating the February race, and he and Henri are planning the race course now."

With a laugh, Frank added, "None of us realized we'd end up in the middle of a movie set."

"Hey, listen," Joe said. "We're planning to get a few days' skiing in the Laurentian Mountains while we're here. Why don't you guys come, too?"

Nancy glanced around to make sure no one was listening. Then, lowering her voice, she said, "We're here on a case."

Frank raised an eyebrow. "Got it," he said quietly. "Why don't you come and meet Henri and Pierre?"

Nancy didn't respond. She was looking past the Hardys at the tense scene between Junot and Politano a dozen yards away.

Henri Dussault, Joe and Frank's host, had his hand on Junot's shoulder and he was talking to the race car driver in a low voice. Junot, sullen and stubborn-looking, finally nodded. He climbed back into his car and backtracked across the ice the way he'd come.

"Well, that's a relief," Bess said. "I wonder if Mr. Politano is planning to shoot that scene now or wait until after lunch."

The director had turned away and was walking across the ice toward the riverbank.

Nancy followed him with her eyes. "Bess?" she said urgently, scanning the ice. "Do you remember where that patch of thin ice was?"

"Sure," Bess said. "Right behind the Danger sign."

"Great," Nancy said. "I see a patch that looks bluish, but I don't see any sign there now. And David is heading straight for it!"

Nancy opened her mouth to yell a warning, but the sound was drowned out by a loud cracking sound. As Nancy watched, horrified, David Politano tried to jump back, but a web of cracks appeared in the ice under his feet, and he lost his balance.

Bess screamed as the director fell backward. A series of popping noises rang out into the crisp, cold air, and water began seeping through the cracked ice under his feet. David Politano's body was flat on the cracking ice, but his boots were soon covered with water.

Within seconds, all the ice would break and his whole body would plunge into the frigid river!

Chapter Two

"HELP!" POLITANO CALLED OUT. He spread his arms and tried to push himself away from the cracking ice, but his gloved hands kept slipping. "Quick, somebody help me!"

"Wait!" Frank yelled. "Everybody, stay back! You'll just crack the ice more!"

As the crew members backed off, Frank lay down flat on the ice and started to slither toward the frightened director.

"The trick is to spread your weight over as much area as you can," Joe explained to Bess and Nancy. He, too, got down on his stomach and followed his brother. "I'll grab Frank's ankles, just in case," he said. "Nancy, Bess, will you hold *my* ankles? Just in case?"

"Sure," Nancy replied. She and Bess immediately dropped down to the ice. They crawled along behind Joe, then each took hold of one of his ankles.

One of the sound crew crawled over to them with a coiled microphone cord in his hand. He gave it to Joe, who tugged at Frank's leg to get his attention, then passed him the cord.

Frank pushed himself up on one elbow and tossed the end of the cord to Politano. "Just hang on to this," he called. "We'll pull you out."

The director grabbed the cord and wrapped it around his wrist a couple of times. Then he clutched it with both hands and held it above his head.

Nancy's heart leapt to her throat as the ice beneath Politano's knees started to give. "Frank, Joe! Quick! Back up!" she shouted.

The director's legs broke through and were covered up to the knees in freezing water. The Hardys yanked on the cord with all their strength and Politano began sliding headfirst toward them and away from the water. A long minute later Politano was safe on solid ice.

"Th-Thanks," the director said through chattering teeth. "That was quick thinking, fellows. I'm glad you were on hand. By the way, do I know you?"

Joe introduced himself and Frank as Emily came running up with a wool blanket. Politano wrapped it around his shoulders, and Frank and Joe walked him toward one of the RVs.

Nancy had begun to pace slowly around the patch of thin ice, her eyes carefully scanning the area.

"What are we looking for?" Bess asked as she and Emily joined Nancy.

"The Danger sign," Nancy replied. "And I think I see it, right over there, wedged in that pile of snow."

The three girls hurried over, and sure enough, the sign was there.

"I thought it might have been blown down," Nancy said. "But I don't think the wind could have piled snow on top of it, too."

Horror showed on Emily's face. "That's terrible! David could have drowned or frozen to death!"

Nancy nodded soberly. "I know. Whoever hid the sign must have done it while we were all distracted by the argument between that race driver and the others. David was unlucky to be the first person to walk that way."

Just then Joe and Frank stepped out of the RV and rejoined the girls.

"What's that?" Frank asked, looking at the sign. "Uh-oh, let me guess. That sign is to warn people about the patch of thin ice."

Joe seemed puzzled. "I never saw any sign."

Frank noticed Emily then and raised an eyebrow at Nancy.

Nancy quickly introduced them and told Frank and Joe why Emily had asked her and Bess to come to Quebec.

"So you think someone's trying to ruin the movie?" Joe asked. "I'd say you're up against someone with a very nasty streak. If you need any help, call. Here's our number at Henri's."

"Thanks," Nancy said, tucking the scrap of paper in her pocket. "Emily, Bess, and I are staying at the Château Frontenac."

"You should see it," Bess added, her eyes shining. "It's this fairy-tale castle with tons of turrets and a fantastic view of the city."

Frank gave a low whistle. "I've seen it from a distance. Pretty classy."

"Most of the movie company is staying there," Emily explained.

"Why don't we all meet there tonight for dinner, then do some sightseeing?" Nancy asked.

"Great," Joe and Frank said at the same moment. Joe glanced back at the sedan they had come in and said, "It looks like Mr. Dussault is hunting for us. We'd better go."

"Seven-thirty, okay?" Frank said as he and Joe took off.

"They seem like nice guys," Emily observed.

"They are," Nancy replied. "They're also very experienced detectives."

Emily gave a little shudder. "I still can't believe somebody deliberately moved that sign," she said. "The other things that have happened were just irritating. They cost us time and money, but this, though—somebody could have been badly hurt . . . or worse."

"Is there anybody who might want to hurt the film?" Nancy asked Emily.

Emily stared thoughtfully out across the river before meeting Nancy's gaze. "Well, there is Billy," she said slowly. "Billy Fitzgerald, the scriptwriter. He also wrote the novel that the movie was taken from, and he's really furious about all the changes that David is making."

"That doesn't sound like a good enough reason to sabotage the film," Bess remarked.

"Not to you, maybe," Emily replied. "But you can never tell with writers. Oops, there's Billy now—the one with the red hair. I think he's looking for me."

The man coming toward them was about five feet ten inches, and overweight, with a thick tweed overcoat flapping around his legs.

A matching tweed cap covered most of his hair, but enough showed to leave no doubt that it was very red.

Nancy couldn't recall noticing him earlier. Could he have removed the Danger sign?

"Emily, darling," Billy said. "Our lord and master has decreed a two-hour recess for lunch. He told me to tell you to pass the word on to the rest of the menials."

"Two hours," Emily repeated. "That's awfully long. Well, I guess he needs time to recover from his accident."

"No doubt. Fearless Leader probably plans to go back to his hotel suite and soak his feet awhile," the writer said sarcastically. "If you ask me, he should soak his head instead."

Emily ignored his comments and turned to Nancy and Bess. "Why don't we go to the Latin Quarter for lunch? I'll round up some of the others. It'll give you a chance to get to know them."

"Excellent thought," Billy said. "Consider me rounded up."

An exasperated expression crossed Emily's face, but Nancy jumped in and said, "Good. I'd love to hear more about your writing." To herself, she added, And find out where you were when that sign was moved.

Understanding dawned in Emily's brown

eyes. "Oh, sure, Billy. Okay. Let me see who else wants to come."

As Emily went for the others, Billy started talking to Nancy and Bess about how incompetent publicity people had kept his most recent novel from becoming a best-seller. Nancy rolled her eyes at Bess. All she wanted him to talk about was where he had been during the scene created by "Snake" Junot.

Nancy and Bess were relieved when Emily came back with two guys. Nancy recognized Dennis Conners, who was wearing a Stetson hat with a feather decoration. The other man was bearded and balding, and he wore a sour expression.

"Dennis Conners, Grant Shulman, meet my cousin Bess and her friend Nancy Drew," Emily said. "I invited them to watch us work."

The two men said hello. Nancy noticed that Bess turned bright red when Dennis Conners shook her hand.

"If that's what you want to call it," Grant Shulman said.

"Maybe you're not working, Grant," Billy said dryly. "But David is keeping *me* busy."

Grant Shulman gave Billy an unfriendly look. "All I meant was that these constant delays are throwing our schedule out the window and costing us a fortune," he said.

"Grant is assistant director on the film," Emily explained to Nancy and Bess. "And you know who Dennis is, of course. I wanted Marguerite to join us, too, but I couldn't find her." She frowned. "Jack's not around, either. I wonder— Never mind. We might as well get going. David said he might join us later."

As they started up the hill, Dennis fell into step beside Bess and Nancy. "Have you ever tried crepes?" he asked. "They're a bit like American pancakes but thinner."

"Oh, yes, I've had them, in Paris," Bess answered smoothly.

Nancy smiled to herself. Way to go, Bess! Her friend wasn't about to let Dennis treat her like a hick.

"That's quite a cowboy hat you're wearing," Bess continued. "Did you grow up on a ranch?"

The young actor smiled. "Not at all," he said. "I'm Canadian, from the province of New Brunswick. But one of these days I'd like to spend some time in the American Southwest. I've had some roles offered me that would take me down that way, but I didn't think they were quite right for my particular talent. Giving the right shape to your career is very important for an actor, you know."

As Dennis continued to talk about his career, Nancy couldn't help thinking he was a little full of himself. Bess seemed completely captivated, though.

Nancy walked ahead to catch up with Emily. "I think Bess is starstruck," Nancy said.

Emily glanced over her shoulder and grinned. "That's the Bess I know. Dennis is kind of self-involved, but if anyone can handle him, Bess can."

Ahead of them Nancy saw that Billy was apparently telling a story, complete with huge arm gestures. Next to him, Grant was walking with his head down and his hands jammed in the pockets of his parka.

"Can you tell me anything about Grant?" Nancy asked.

Emily shrugged. "I don't know a whole lot about him. As I said, he's the assistant director. He's not well-known, but he has done some directing on his own. David's been his friend since they were at film school together."

"He and Billy don't seem to get along."

"Grant's moody. He likes to keep to himself. And Billy—well, you just spent five minutes with him, so you know. I'm just as glad that he's not at the Château Frontenac with the rest of us. He and I had quite a fight about it."

"Why?" Nancy asked.

"Billy insisted on getting a room at a little hotel here in the Latin Quarter," Emily explained. "He said his artistic impulses were being smothered in such a crowded, touristy place as the Frontenac."

The street narrowed and was lined with old houses made of stone and brick. Some were freshly painted, but others looked as if they hadn't been touched in a hundred years.

Emily pointed to one with a sign that read Auberge des Remparts. "That's the hotel where Billy is staying," she said. "The place we're going for lunch is just around the corner."

A moment later Nancy and Emily joined Billy and Grant outside a rough stone house with small-paned windows. The only clue that it was a restaurant was a wooden sign over the door.

" 'À la Vieille Bretagne,' " Nancy read aloud while the group waited for Bess and Dennis to catch up. "That means 'In old Brittany,' right?"

"Sounds good to me," Emily said with a shrug. "I haven't a clue. How have you liked your visit to the set so far, by the way?"

Great! Nancy thought. Emily had given her the perfect lead-in to question Billy. "I know moviemaking is supposed to be exciting, but I had no idea it could be *so* exciting!" she said. "What was that driver so upset about?" she asked Billy.

"Junot, you mean?" the writer replied distractedly. "I missed seeing it. I was in the office trailer, grinding out some boring script changes, as specified by you know who."

He looked down the street and added, "Lucky us. Here comes our fearless leader now."

Nancy turned just as David Politano got out of a limousine that had stopped beside them. Bess and Dennis caught up to the group then, too.

"Billy?" said Politano. "I'm sorry to interrupt your lunch, but I think the scene we're scheduled to shoot this afternoon still needs work."

"What!" the scriptwriter exclaimed. "You've got to be—"

David Politano took Billy's elbow and led him aside. The two men had a discussion that grew steadily louder and more heated.

"I'm sorry," David finally snapped angrily. "I insist. The dialogue has to be rewritten."

Billy's face was as red as his hair, and his fists were clenched into tight balls at his sides. "You're hopeless, Politano," Billy shouted. "This would have been a great day if only you'd ended up where you were headed—at the bottom of the river, with the rest of the slime!"

Chapter Three

FRANK DECIDED it was a real kick to be riding up the middle of a frozen river. The tires spun out a little even with their heavy metal studs, and Frank glanced back to see his brother's reaction.

Joe was grinning, itching to get behind the wheel. That was Joe—all action.

"What a wonderful coincidence that your friends should be in Quebec just now," Dussault said from the front seat. "I was sorry to pull you away, but we have to get back. The Auto Federation is making a film this afternoon—a commercial for the Carnival, featuring André Junot in his race car."

"The race car driver we just saw back there?" Joe asked.

"That's right," said Dussault, nodding. "He was last year's ice-racing champion. He is very popular with the crowds."

"He didn't seem very popular with anyone on the movie set," Frank observed.

Dussault gave a shrug. "Junot is not always tender with the feelings of others," he said. "But he *is* the champion, so he is an important spokesperson for the sport."

Just ahead, Frank could see the old boat house that the Auto Federation was using as a garage and headquarters for the Carnival's ice-racing event. A little knot of people was standing on the ice in front of the low building, near Junot's race car.

"The reporters and photographers are gathering already," said Pierre Desmoulins. "Wait until they find out about our surprise guest."

"Do we have a surprise guest?" Henri Dussault asked.

"We certainly do," Pierre replied with a smile. "When I heard that the film company was taking a two-hour break, I invited Marguerite Laforet to have a sandwich with us as we watch Junot's commercial being made."

"Ah," said Dussault. "And she accepted? Wonderful!"

Pierre explained to Frank and Joe, "Marguerite plays the female lead in the film. She is much loved in Quebec. *Dangerous Loves* will give her a chance to find a wider audience—especially if the movie is shown in the U.S."

The foursome got out of the car near the boat house and joined the crowd. Junot was being interviewed by a young woman in a trench coat. "On the ice, no one goes faster than me—no one!" Junot declared.

"With the mouth, he is even faster," someone near Frank muttered.

The man who had spoken couldn't have been much older than thirty, but his face was deeply lined. Frank remembered seeing him on the movie set. What was he doing here?

Noticing Frank, the man smiled and spoke to him. "I watched your rescue of Monsieur Politano a little while ago." As the man stepped closer to him, Frank noticed that he favored his right leg. "Congratulations. It is not so easy to keep one's wits when there is sudden danger. I am François Volnay."

"Hi," Frank said. "I'm Frank Hardy and this is my brother, Joe." Just then Pierre Desmoulins came up behind François Volnay and slapped him on the back.

"Well, François, how is it going?" Pierre asked. Turning to the Hardys, he added,

"François is one of the *real* champions of ice racing. Not like some, who are maybe better at bragging than driving."

"Why do you allow it, Pierre?" Volnay demanded angrily. "Why do you give Snake so much notice? As a member of the Auto Federation, you should stop him, not push him forward!"

"What can we do?" said Pierre. "As long as Snake Junot is champion, the reporters will flock to him. Believe me, the day after he loses, he will be forgotten."

"I hope so," François muttered. He gestured toward the boat house entrance, where Henri Dussault was beckoning to him. "Excuse me, please," François said. "I am needed."

As François Volnay limped away, Pierre said, "What a pity. He has never been the same since his accident last year."

"Was he a race car driver?" asked Joe. "Is that how he got that limp?"

Pierre nodded. "During the Winter Carnival race, he lost control and crashed. He and Junot were fighting for the lead at the time."

No wonder François was so bitter about Junot, Frank thought. That kind of defeat had to be hard. "François still seems very active, though," he commented.

"For the instant, he is occupied," Pierre told him. "He is working as technical advisor on the film where you just saw your friends. Ordinarily, he just has a small job with Henri's company. Henri offered the job out of friendship, to give François something to occupy himself. It doesn't pay much, and I know François must miss the thrill of racing. Excuse me, I too have things to do before Junot starts his run. There is a table set up with food just inside the boat house. Help yourselves."

Frank glanced over at the crowd around Junot again. The driver was still talking in rapid-fire French. The only word Frank could make out was *champion.* It seemed to come up in every other sentence.

Suddenly there was a stir in the crowd. Marguerite Laforet had just arrived. Her face was flushed as she hurried over to Junot and said breathlessly, "I'm sorry to be late. I was afraid I would have missed everything."

Junot kissed her on each cheek. "You have missed nothing," he declared. "*I* am here. That is everything, no?"

He put his arm around her shoulders and turned to face the TV cameras.

"Excuse me, coming through!" a man said urgently behind Frank and Joe.

They stepped aside as a tall, skinny guy with spiked blond hair hurried past. He had two cameras around his neck and an equipment bag over one shoulder. He clicked off half a dozen shots of Marguerite and Junot, then glanced back.

"Hi," he said to Frank and Joe. "You're the two guys who rescued David Politano from the ice, aren't you? That was impressive."

"It was nothing any superhero wouldn't have done," Joe said.

Frank groaned. "Spoken like a true egomaniac, little brother," he said.

The tall guy laughed and held out his hand. "I'm Jack Parmenter. I saw you talking to Nancy and Bess, too. I'm a friend of Bess's cousin Emily."

"Are you part of the film company?" asked Joe after he and Frank introduced themselves.

Jack raised one of his cameras. "I'm the still photographer. That's why I'm here. Anything that Marguerite does is part of my job," he said, grinning. "I'd better get back to work. See you guys later."

Jack disappeared into the crowd.

"Frank, Joe."

Frank saw Henri beckoning them over. He was standing near the big double doors of the boat house with a young man who had short blond hair, hazel eyes, and a closely trimmed beard. The younger man was wearing boots, black jeans, and a heavy motorcycle jacket.

"This is Brent Moore," Henri told the Hardys when they joined him. "Brent is one of the very best of our younger racing drivers. He should be the favorite to win the Carnival race this year."

"Should be?" Frank repeated. "What do you mean?"

Dussault gestured toward the reporters around Junot. "André has a flair for promoting himself," he said. "As a result, the press has not paid as much attention to Brent as they should. But that will change soon, I am certain."

"Monsieur Dussault? Telephone," someone called out from the door of the boat house.

"He's a great guy," Brent said after Dussault excused himself and went inside. "He'd do just about anything to promote race car driving. But I'm afraid he's wrong about me."

Frank gave Brent a curious look. "You don't think you'll win this year?"

"Oh, not that. With a little luck, I can beat Snake," Brent replied with an easy smile. "But that won't make the local press like me."

"Why's that?" asked Joe.

"The media favors locals," Brent told the Hardys. "I'm not from Quebec. I'm not even French Canadian. My grandparents came to Canada from Ireland."

"Does that matter?" Frank asked.

The racing driver nodded. "Around here, it certainly does," he said. "French Canadians are very proud of their heritage. Snake may not be very nice, but he is *Québecois.* That's enough to make him a hit with the fans."

"Pardon, pardon!" Two men began to push Junot's car out onto the ice. A third crew member reached in through the window and steered.

The crowd of reporters and camera people moved out of the way. Junot was still standing with his arm around Marguerite. Frank thought that she looked relieved when he moved away.

Junot started for the car but paused when a young woman in a pink jumpsuit called out to him from the boat house entrance. She ran up to him, then slapped his face.

"Uh-oh," Brent murmured. "Snake's got romantic troubles."

"Do you know who she is?" Joe asked.

"Her name's Danielle Rocheville," Brent replied. "This is her first year racing. I didn't know she and Snake had a thing going."

"You thought I wouldn't know!" Danielle accused Junot. She was petite with a curvy build and auburn hair. "You thought I wouldn't see! But I was here! I saw!"

Junot seemed to be searching for a way to escape. Frank noticed the reporters who were nudging one another to get their miniature tape recorders closer to Danielle and Junot.

"You had your arms around her," Danielle continued. "In front of everyone! You dare to humiliate me in public!" She burst into tears.

Frank was relieved when Pierre Desmoulins forced his way through the crowd and hurried over to the couple. "Danielle, this is not the time," he said. "Please go inside."

Danielle looked as if she was about to yell at Pierre, too, but then she turned and stormed off toward the boat house.

"André?" Pierre continued. "The film crew is ready for you to make your run now. The light is good."

Junot bent down to examine one of the front tires. Then, glimpsing the crowd pressed eagerly around him, he apparently changed his mind.

The director spoke up then. "All right, Junot, go down the river beyond that bridge, turn around, and come back here at full speed," he said. "Are you ready?"

With a last grin for the cameras, Junot vaulted through the open window of his car, put on his helmet, and fastened the shoulder harness. With a nonchalant wave, he swerved into the center of the ice and sped down the river toward the bridge. A moment later he was out of sight around the curve.

"Well," Joe said. "He sure—"

He was cut off as a flash of orange lit up the

frozen river. An instant later a loud boom reverberated back to them.

"What!" Joe exclaimed.

Frank had a sick feeling in the pit of his stomach. From beyond the bridge a column of gray-black smoke billowed up to smudge the pale winter sky.

"Come on," he said urgently, grabbing Joe's shoulder. "Junot's car just exploded!"

Chapter Four

JOE TOOK OFF after Frank, running down the river. Adrenaline pounded through his veins, but it was hard to run on the ice.

He and Frank had gone only about a hundred yards when an emergency truck sped past. Seconds later a horn beeped just behind them. It was Henri and Pierre in Henri's car. Joe and Frank scrambled into the backseat.

Joe's mouth dropped open in horror when the sedan rounded the curve in the river and he saw the flaming ruin of Junot's car. Two men were aiming a stream of foam at the fire, but the flames roared on. The air over the car shimmered with the heat. Beneath it, a shallow pool of melted ice was spreading.

As soon as the sedan stopped, everyone jumped out and raced over to the emergency team of four.

"Junot? Is he—" Dussault couldn't bring himself to finish the sentence.

"He never made it out of the car," one of the men replied.

Joe's stomach turned over.

An ambulance came speeding down to the riverbank, lights flashing. Dussault watched it for a moment, then said, "Come, Pierre. There is nothing we can do here, and the press will have many questions to ask us back at the boat house." Shaking his head sadly, he added, "I wish we had some answers.

"Pierre, will you have what is left of André's car brought back to the Federation garage? I will tell my best team of mechanics to look it over. If nothing else, we may learn how to prevent another tragedy like this one."

"I'm not sure—" Pierre began. Then he glanced at Dussault's set face and said, "Yes, of course. I'll see to it right away."

Joe exchanged a sober look with Frank. Their vacation in romantic Quebec was certainly getting off to a grim start.

* * *

Nancy, Bess, and Emily were threading through the extras on the riverbank to head for David Politano, who was pacing in front of his trailer. When the girls approached, he wheeled around.

"Well?" he demanded.

Emily blinked nervously. "I'm sorry, David," she said. "No one knows where Marguerite is."

"How am I supposed to make a film without my female lead?" he growled.

Emily studied her clipboard. "I guess we could skip to scene forty-nine. That scene is just Dennis."

"I don't understand this!" David roared. "Didn't I say two hours? Didn't everyone hear me say it?"

Not waiting for Emily to answer, the director pressed his hands to his temples and said, "All these delays are bringing on a migraine. I'm going inside to lie down. Come and get me the moment she shows up."

"Whew!" said Bess after he'd stalked off. "Is he always like that?"

Emily grinned. "No. Sometimes he gets *really* mad. Quick, let's get out of here before he thinks of something else."

"Look, there's Billy," Nancy said. "Do you think he finished those revisions David wanted?"

"I certainly hope so," Emily replied. "We don't need another explosion like the one at the restaurant. For a minute there I thought they were actually going to punch each other out."

"I think I'll try to talk to Billy again," Nancy said. "I'm going to find out exactly what he knows about that missing Danger sign and the other accidents."

Nancy followed the screenwriter to a trailer that was set up as a lounge for the company. Inside were a small couch, some chairs, a card table, and a compact kitchen area. Billy was drawing a cup of coffee from the big urn on the counter when she came in.

"Hi. Want one?" he offered, holding up his coffee.

"No, thanks," Nancy replied. "I had some tea with lunch. It's too bad you couldn't stay. The crepes were delicious."

"With King Politano there, I doubt I would have enjoyed myself," Billy told her.

"You two don't get along," Nancy observed.

Billy gave a shout of laughter. "That's the understatement of the year!"

"From what Emily has told me, this film has had a lot more than its share of accidents and delays," Nancy continued, changing the subject. "I mean, the reason David almost fell through that patch of thin ice is because the Danger sign was mysteriously removed."

"I never noticed it," Billy said with a shrug. "Someone on the crew must have knocked it over, then was too scared to 'fess up. David is not the forgiving sort."

"It almost seems as if somebody wants to *make* this film fail," she pressed.

"The same thought crossed my mind," Billy admitted. "But in the end, I put it down to incompetence, not malice. Who'd want to see the film destroyed? Not me. I may hate what David is doing to my story, but to have my book filmed is a big step in my career. Of course, there's . . ." Billy's voice trailed off, and he took a sip of his coffee.

"What?" Nancy asked, studying his face carefully.

"Nothing. Just that—well, I have it on very good authority that dear Dennis was recently offered a juicy role in a Hollywood movie. He's going to have to turn it down, because the shooting schedule overlaps with our little epic here in Quebec. But if this project goes down the tubes . . . Well, we all know that Dennis would walk over his grandmother in spiked boots to break into Hollywood."

That fit with Nancy's impression of Dennis from lunch. He had spent the whole time talking about himself and his career. On the other hand, Billy might be trying to divert suspicion away from himself.

Just then the door to the trailer flew open, and Emily came in.

"Nancy, there you are!" she exclaimed. "Something awful has happened! Marguerite and Jack were at some publicity shoot for the Carnival. Come quickly!"

Nancy hurried after Emily. Down at the river's edge fifteen or twenty people were gathered around Marguerite.

"It just blew up, like that?" someone asked.

"Like that," the actress replied. Her arms sketched a mushroom cloud in the air. *"Boom!* It was horrible!"

Nancy and Emily joined Bess at the edge of the crowd. "What is it?" Nancy asked.

"That Junot who was here this morning," Bess said shakily. "His car caught on fire an hour ago. He's dead."

Nancy felt the blood drain from her face. "That's horrible!"

"It sure is," Jack said, walking up to the girls. "I didn't actually see the explosion, but I got to the scene soon afterward and saw the results." His shudder said more than any words could have.

Nancy was startled as the door to David

Politano's trailer banged open. "What is all that infernal racket?" the director demanded, stalking over to the group.

As Emily explained what had happened, David looked more annoyed than upset. Then he went over to Marguerite.

"My dear," he said, taking both her hands. "What a terrible ordeal you've been through. But I think the best thing for you, the *only* thing, is to throw yourself into your work. Don't you agree?"

Nancy struggled to keep her temper. Could David really be as heartless as he sounded? A man had just died in a horrible accident, and all he cared about was getting his movie finished!

Marguerite hesitated, then said, "Yes, I suppose so."

David released one of her hands, so that he could pat the other one. "Good," he said. "Now, off to makeup. We don't have more than an hour of usable daylight left, and I intend to take advantage of every bit of it."

"Can you believe this guy?" Bess commented, shaking her head. "No wonder no one likes him."

"The assistant director doesn't seem to share his enthusiasm," Nancy said.

She nodded to her right, where Grant

Shulman was sitting on a canvas chair, a plaid scarf wrapped over his chin and a morose expression on his face.

Grant raised his head and noticed Nancy and Bess watching him. He gave them a tired smile, then turned to Emily as she walked up to him.

"Grant, this just came for you." She handed him a red, white, and blue Express Mail envelope about the size of a school notebook. "The hotel sent someone over with it. They thought it might be urgent."

"Thanks," he said. He took the envelope, glanced quickly at the contents, and hurried off in the direction of one of the RVs.

"It must be urgent if he's leaving the set," Emily said. "Grant's in charge of setting up this next scene. He might not know if something's wrong now." She shook her head.

Nancy moved aside to let a crew member set up a tall stand with a metal reflector on top. At the riverbank, on the top of a small slope, other stagehands were pushing Dennis's red race car into place and positioning cameras, lights, and reflectors nearby.

"I never knew making a film was so complicated," Bess remarked. "There's so much to take care of before they can even start shooting."

"What's happening in this scene?" Nancy asked Emily.

"Dennis's character is about to drive off to the prerace time trials," Emily explained. "Marguerite knows how important he has become to her, and she wants to show him how she feels. She can't let the people around her see it because she's supposed to be engaged to the guy who's Dennis's competitor."

Dennis and Marguerite emerged from their dressing rooms and took up positions facing each other on the edge of the ice. Dennis was in his white racing coverall again, and his helmet dangled from one hand. Marguerite was wearing a hooded fur coat. A short distance up the slope of the riverbank, extras in mechanics' and drivers' costumes stood near the parked race car.

"All right, boys and girls," David said. "Our lovers have their dialogue, in tight close-up. Then we dolly back and widen, as Dennis goes up to his car and climbs in."

The guy with the bullhorn called for silence, the lights blinked on, and the cameras started to roll.

Bess clutched Nancy's arm excitedly when Marguerite began to speak her lines. On the surface, Marguerite's words were casual, but she managed to communicate both her attraction and her doubts through them.

Like everyone else on the set, Nancy was captivated by her superb acting.

Then a slight movement caught Nancy's eye. She looked up and gasped. Dennis's empty race car had begun to roll down the slope.

Marguerite and Dennis were directly in its path!

Chapter Five

"Dennis! Marguerite! Look out!" Nancy shouted. Her cries were picked up by the extras standing near the car.

Nancy took off toward the actors. "The car! It's moving!" she continued to yell.

It was rolling faster now. Marguerite had turned to stare at it, open-mouthed, and froze in place like a deer caught in a car's headlights.

Nancy dashed the last few yards, grabbed Marguerite around the waist, and pulled her out of the car's path. She had reached for Dennis with her other arm but missed him. A split second later the car brushed up against

Nancy as it went by. Nancy toppled to her hands and knees, and Marguerite sprawled on the ground beside her.

Where was Dennis? Nancy pushed herself up to look around. Dennis had managed to jump onto the hood of the rolling car and was clinging to the bars of the windshield. Nancy gasped as a microphone boom fell across the car top, narrowly missing him.

Then, as suddenly as it had started, the crisis was over. The car, now on level ice, bumped across the track that had been laid for the camera, slowed down and stopped.

For a long moment no one moved. Finally, Dennis climbed down from the hood of the car, brushed off his coveralls, and said loudly, "David, I'm sure my contract states that I am *not* supposed to do my own stunts."

Everyone burst out laughing, except Nancy, who was too troubled by the near-miss to join in. Nancy got to her feet and headed up the slope to the spot where the car had been parked. Half a dozen extras were standing in a group. As Nancy drew near, she heard one of them say, "I don't know how it happened, I tell you. All I did was lean against the fender, and suddenly it started to move!"

David charged up the slope just then. "Who put that car in place?" he shouted.

After a silence that seemed to last forever,

one of the stagehands stepped forward. "I did, Mr. Politano," he said.

"You're fired," the director proclaimed.

"Just one moment," said someone in a deep voice. Nancy recognized François Volnay, the technical advisor. He limped over to David and said, "I checked over the car only a few moments before you started filming. I assure you that the hand brake was set."

David threw his hands up in the air. "Next you're going to tell me that I imagined that car started rolling! From now on, don't just set the brake—put something in front of the wheels."

With that, the director stomped off in the direction of his trailer, pausing only to tell Emily to cancel the rest of the day's shooting.

Nancy thought quickly. If François Volnay was right, and the brake had been set, then someone had to have released it.

She went over to François. "I don't understand," she said naively. "If the brake was set, how could the car move?"

"It couldn't," he replied. "Not with the brake set all the way. On the other hand, if it had been set only partway, it would slow the car but not stop it."

Nancy saw that the car was still sitting on the ice where it had come to a halt.

"Can we go see?" she asked.

"Why not?" he said.

When they reached the car, Nancy leaned in the driver's window. The hand brake stuck up a little from the transmission tunnel but not much. "Is that the way the brake was when you checked it?" she asked Volnay.

He scratched his chin. "I think it was set harder than that, but I am not sure."

That wasn't much help. Nancy stretched her arm toward the hand brake, but her fingertips didn't quite reach it. In order to release the brake, she'd have to climb in through the window. There was no way she, or anyone else, could do that without being noticed.

So either the stagehand hadn't set the brake hard enough, or someone with longer arms than hers had secretly loosened it.

Maybe François himself had done it. No one would have noticed him, because his job gave him the right to fiddle with the cars.

Nancy straightened up and turned to ask the former race driver a few more questions, but he wasn't there. She decided she was being overly suspicious. After all, she didn't know of any reason François Volnay would want to sabotage *Dangerous Loves.*

"Nancy! You were wonderful!"

Bess hurried over, arm in arm with Marguerite. "When you ran in front of the car, I thought I was going to die! My heart was in my throat!"

"I haven't thanked you," Marguerite added. "You saved my life."

Nancy felt embarrassed. "You would have been okay. The car wasn't moving very fast."

Marguerite shook her head. "Bess warned me that you would make light of this. In any case, I do thank you," Marguerite said. Checking her watch, she added, "I must go now. I am very glad that David has called off the rest of the filming. Today has been terrible, and I must look my best tomorrow—it's my wedding day."

Nancy and Bess exchanged a long, puzzled look.

When they found Emily, they asked about Marguerite's wedding. She burst out laughing. "Tomorrow *is* her wedding day—in the movie. We're shooting at the Notre Dame Basilica.

"I've got a lot to finish before I can leave," Emily said. "You guys might as well go back to the hotel without me."

"Don't forget," Bess said. "We're having dinner tonight with Joe and Frank."

"The lobby of the Frontenac at seven-thirty," Emily replied. "Jack and I will be there."

"I could stay here forever," Nancy said, pausing on the terrace in front of the Château Frontenac to admire the view that evening.

She, Emily, Jack, Bess, and the Hardys were just leaving the hotel on their way to dinner.

"The view is fantastic," Frank agreed, standing next to Nancy at the guardrail. "If you don't mind the height."

Below them, straight down a sheer cliff, lights sparkled on the streets and in the windows of the buildings in the oldest section of the city, the Petit-Champlain Quarter. Just beyond this, the ice-choked Saint Lawrence River was bathed in a yellow glow from a three-quarter moon.

"You'd better get used to that," said Emily, her breath coming out in small white puffs. "Because the restaurant where we're eating is right down there." She leaned over the railing and pointed down and to the left, where a steep stairway led down the cliff. "On Breakneck Stairs."

Bess eyed the stairway in disbelief. "You don't expect us to walk down there, do you?" she asked.

"That's the only way you're going to get your dinner," Jack put in with a mischievous grin.

"Isn't there some kind of elevator that goes down to the Lower Town?" Joe asked. "Henri said something about it."

"Actually, it's called a funicular. The entrance is just up ahead." Emily pointed to a small building at the edge of the cliff. "We can't ride it now, though, since the restaurant is actually *on* Breakneck Stairs."

Nancy found Breakneck Stairs just as steep, scary, and picturesque as its name suggested. Old houses lined either side and seemed to reach for each other over the stairs.

Inside the restaurant the proprietor led the group to a round table in a little alcove near a fireplace. On the stone walls, antique copper cooking pots glimmered in the firelight.

"Bess tells me that you and your brother are terrific detectives," Emily said, turning to Joe and Frank after the waiter had left with their orders.

"Only the best," said Joe.

"With the possible exception of a certain red-haired sleuth," Frank added. When he smiled at Nancy, she could feel herself blush.

"We're on vacation now, though," Frank continued. "We were thinking about going skiing, and maybe taking a snowmobile trek for a couple of days."

"Sounds like fun," Jack said. "I'd love to come along and take pictures."

Nancy snapped her fingers. "That reminds me, Jack. I wanted to ask about the photos you took on the set today. Could I take a look at them sometime soon? They might contain some important clues about who's sabotaging the movie."

"Sure. I'll probably develop them and make contact sheets later tonight," Jack replied. "You can see them tomorrow morning."

"You have your own darkroom here, Jack?" Joe asked.

Jack nodded. "I met a photographer in Quebec named Mike Adams. He has his own studio, so I made a deal with him to share it. He gives me a hand sometimes on the set."

The waiter brought their appetizer, a big tray of pâté, bread, and fruit.

"Do you have any idea who could be sabotaging the movie?" Frank asked, popping a grape into his mouth.

"Suspects are easy," Nancy said, giving him a rueful smile. "It's proof that's hard to get. But we've got a couple of candidates. Billy Fitzgerald, the screenwriter, seems to hate the director, maybe enough to try to sabotage the film. And I hear that the male lead in the movie has recently gotten the kind of offer he's always dreamed about. But he can't take it, because of his contract to do *Dangerous Loves.*"

Bess stared at Nancy. "Who are you talking about? You can't mean Dennis!"

"Well—" Nancy began.

Joe shot Bess a sly smile. "Not that you have

any personal interest in the guy, right, Bess?" he teased.

Ignoring Joe's remark, Bess turned to Nancy and demanded, "Who told you that? Never mind, I can guess. It was Billy, wasn't it? He'd say anything to throw suspicion off himself."

"Dennis told a lot of us about the offer," Emily put in. "He tried to make a joke of it, but I could see that he was really upset."

"That doesn't mean he'd try to wreck *Dangerous Loves,*" Bess insisted.

"No, it doesn't," agreed Nancy. "And as for the last incident with the car, I'm not sure I see *how* he could have pulled it off. I do have a suspect who could have released the brake, though—the film's racing expert, François Volnay."

"Hey, we know him," Frank said. "A guy with a limp, right? He used to be a champion driver."

Nancy nodded. "That's him. He had the best chance to release the brake on the stunt car this afternoon. But I can't see *why* he'd want to delay the film."

"I think I can," Jack said. "Em, is Volnay on per diem?"

Emily thought for a moment before answering. "I think so. And if I remember correctly, it's pretty generous, too."

"You mean, he gets paid by the day," Nancy

said. "So the longer it takes to finish the film, the more he makes. If he needs money badly, that might be enough of a motive."

"He probably does need money," Joe put in. "Pierre told us that his job at Dussault Motors doesn't pay much."

"Pierre is Pierre Desmoulins," Frank explained, turning to the others. "He's the guy from the Auto Federation we were with today when we saw you. If you want, we can ask him a few questions," he offered. "But I have to say, I get the feeling people have a lot of respect for François."

They continued to discuss the case until the waiter arrived with the main course. "I must have died and gone to heaven!" Bess exclaimed. "My goose looks too delicious to be real."

After that, everybody was more interested in eating than in discussing mysteries.

"Hey, I've got a great idea," Jack said after dinner. "Let's take the funicular back up to the Place d'Armes, then go for a ride in a calèche. That's a horse-drawn carriage."

Nancy soon found herself sitting between Frank and Joe, on the rear-facing seat of the old carriage that clip-clopped through the narrow streets of the Upper Town. A thick, warm blanket covered their legs and feet. Emily, Jack, and Bess were settled in across from them. The coachman kept turning around to point out landmarks.

As the carriage came even with the mouth of a narrow street, the driver turned around to explain. "This is the Rue du Trésor. Treasury Street. Quebec's artists exhibit their work on the sidewalks here during the summer and—"

Suddenly there was a flash and a loud bang, right under the horse's hooves. Nancy grabbed Frank's arm as the horse gave a leap. The driver tried to turn around and rein it in, but the sudden jerking threw him off balance and down onto the street. The calèche had no driver!

The frenzied horse galloped forward, pulling the swaying carriage into the Place d'Armes. Nancy turned around to look ahead and gasped. On the far side of the square was the edge of the cliff where they had stood and admired the view earlier. Their carriage was headed straight for it.

Only a railing stood between them and a two-hundred-foot drop to the Lower Town.

Chapter Six

Joe got to his feet and braced himself against the side of the wildly swaying carriage. The frightened horse had dodged around the fountain in the center of the Place d'Armes and was dashing blindly for the edge of the cliff. It was only a matter of seconds before they would plunge over the side.

"Everybody, jump!" Bess screamed.

"Bess, don't!" Emily said urgently. "The carriage wheels could run over you!"

Fighting to keep his balance, Joe climbed over the carriage seat to the driver's perch. He leaned out over the footrest and looked down.

The horses reins were dragging on the ground, far out of reach. Just his luck.

He didn't know how the idea occurred to him or what made him follow the crazy urge. All of a sudden he found himself stepping down over the front edge of the carriage onto the thick wooden bar to which the horse's harness was attached.

He didn't give himself time to think. Steadying himself by holding the front edge of the carriage with one hand, he gathered his strength, then sprang.

He landed squarely on the horse's back. The startled horse lunged to one side, and Joe had to grab the leather belly band to keep from falling. Once he recovered his balance, he reached down and grasped the horse's reins. The cliff edge was only fifteen feet away now.

"Whoa, there," Joe called. He yanked back on the reins hard and pulled the horse sharply to the left.

To his relief, the horse went left, away from the cliff edge, then slowed to a walk. Joe slid off the horse's back and held it steady.

"Everybody out," he called. "Fun's over."

Everyone looked pretty shaken. The coachman ran up, breathless, and took the bridle of the trembling horse. He started stroking its muzzle and soothing it in French.

"I am very sorry," he said. "Never has he run like that before."

"Something startled him," Frank said, frowning. "And I have a hunch what it was. Let's take a look at the street back there."

After searching the pavement for a minute, Bess called out, "Hey, everybody, I think I found something."

Jogging over to her, they saw a fragment of gray cardboard in Bess's palm. It was a little smaller than a postage stamp and had ragged edges. One side was covered with red tissue paper printed with tiny white stars. The other side was blackened.

"Is this what I think it is?" Bess asked.

Nancy took the piece of cardboard from Bess and held it to her nose. "It sure is," she replied. "It's what's left of a firecracker. Someone must have thrown it, deliberately trying to spook our horse."

"But who would do a thing like that?" Jack asked. "We could have been killed!"

"Here's something that may help to answer that question," Frank said, rejoining them. "I just found it a few yards down that side street."

He showed them a Stetson hat with a feather ornament. "There can't be too many people in Quebec who wear fancy cowboy hats," Joe added, laughing. "With a little luck, we'll track down the owner."

"We won't need luck," said Emily. "I know that hat. It belongs to Dennis Conners."

Bess scowled. "Well, what if it *is* his?" she said. "Somebody may have planted it there—somebody who wanted to throw suspicion on him."

"Maybe," said Nancy. She took the hat from Frank. "But I'll be interested to hear what Dennis has to say about it tomorrow."

Emily yawned, then glanced at her watch. "It's almost midnight, guys," she said. "I'd better get some sleep. I've got a lot to do tomorrow morning, before we start shooting."

"Including having breakfast with Nancy and me," said Bess. "Remember, Em, you promised to show us the most delicious croissants in Quebec."

Nancy turned to Frank and Joe. "I'll give you a call tomorrow," she promised, "and tell you what Dennis has to say for himself."

"I can't believe I'm actually up and awake at six-thirty in the morning," Bess said the next morning as she and Nancy left their room. "Did I remember to get dressed?"

"You did," Nancy reassured her. "We look pretty good, if I do say so myself."

They walked down the fourth-floor hall to Emily's room and knocked on the door. "Come in!" Emily called, her voice muffled.

They found her at the table she was using as a desk, wearing jeans and a sweatshirt. The telephone was cradled against her shoulder. She waved them in, then rummaged through one of her stacks of papers.

"Well, *that's* taken care of," Emily said a moment later, hanging up the phone. She crossed off an item in her memo book.

"What is?" Bess asked.

"I had to find a stunt driver to replace Snake Junot," Emily explained. "And we had to have him today, too. Luckily, I was able to track down a very good driver, Brent Moore. We'll have to pay him extra, because of the short notice, but at least we won't have to change the shooting schedule."

Emily scanned her memo book again, then put it in her shoulder bag. "Okay, let's go. I hope you're ready for the best croissants in Quebec."

"My stomach is growling already," said Bess.

As the three girls walked along the street, Emily glanced at the shopping bag in Nancy's hand. "What's in there?" she asked.

Bess frowned and answered for Nancy. "Dennis's hat. I still say you're wrong about him, Nan. Just because we found it near where our horse was startled doesn't prove anything, you know," she added defensively.

"I know it doesn't," Nancy said. "But when I give it back to him, I certainly mean to ask him for an explanation."

At the end of the block the street opened onto a large park. Surprisingly, trailers and RVs from the movie company were lined up along one side of the street. Crew members were unloading hampers filled with lighting equipment and wheeling them across to the steps of a large, ornate church.

"That's the Notre Dame Basilica," Emily said. "It's almost three hundred fifty years old. Just wait until you see the inside. It's filled with paintings and statues from the days when Quebec was a French settlement."

"Why are they setting up the lights on the steps?" asked Bess.

"We're shooting exteriors this morning," Emily told her. "What's happening in the story is, Marguerite is just about to marry the man she always thought she loved. But Dennis comes speeding up in his race car, dashes into the church, and begs her to run away with him. She agrees, they jog down the steps to the car, and the car roars off as the wedding guests come out to see what's going on."

"It isn't really Dennis driving the car?" Bess said.

Emily rolled her eyes. "Not a chance. The insurance company would have fits! That's why I was so desperate to find another driver. Come on. The place we're going is just a block away."

A few minutes later they entered a café with green double doors. All at once Nancy felt as if she had been miraculously transported to Paris.

The girls took a table near the window. When the waiter offered them menus, Bess said, "I already know exactly what I want—croissants and a café au lait."

Nancy and Emily ordered the same. A few minutes later a waiter returned with big pitchers of coffee and steamed milk, and little ceramic dishes of butter and fresh strawberry jam.

"What are those?" Bess demanded, peering down at the long, straight rolls in the basket the waiter placed in front of them. "I wanted croissants!"

"These are what we call *croissants-torpilles,*" the waiter replied. "Torpedo-shaped croissants. They are a specialty here in Quebec."

"Oh?" Bess broke off the end of one, buttered it and added a bit of jam. When she bit into it, her face lit up. "It's fantastic!" she exclaimed. "I may never go back to croissant-shaped croissants again!"

Nancy took the two pitchers and poured streams of milk and coffee into each of the cups. After taking a couple of sips, she said, "I've been thinking about what happened last night."

"You're not the only one," Bess replied, dipping her croissant into her coffee and taking another bite. "I had nightmares about our carriage going over that cliff."

"Whoever threw the firecracker had no way of knowing that the coachman would fall off and the horse would bolt," Nancy pointed out. "He or she probably just wanted to frighten us. But what I'm wondering is who the attack was aimed at."

"Why, us, of course," Bess replied.

"Yes, but which of us?" Nancy asked. "You and me? Nobody knows why we're really here. Joe and Frank aren't even on a case. Why would anybody be after them?" Nancy took another sip of coffee. "Which means that you and Jack were probably the targets," she told Emily.

"Oh, no!" Bess cried. "Nancy, are you sure?"

Nancy nodded. "Pretty sure. Emily, your work is very important to keeping *Dangerous Loves* on schedule, isn't it?"

Emily nodded blankly. "There's a lot of coordination and planning that has to be done, sure."

"If something scared you enough to make you quit, it would cause a major delay, wouldn't it?" Nancy continued.

"Well—yes," Emily replied. "But I'm not planning to quit."

"Of course not," Nancy said. She brushed her reddish blond hair back from her face and took a bite of her croissant before adding, "But from now on, Emily, I think you should be a lot more careful. It looks to me as if you've become a target."

"Hey, Joe, I was thinking," Frank said, as he, Joe, and Henri Dussault were just finishing breakfast in Mr. Dussault's large oak-paneled dining room. "What do you say we check out the cross-country skiing on the Plains of Abraham today."

Joe nodded. "Sounds good to me."

Henri looked up from the newspaper he was reading and said, "I would like to show you something of our countryside, as soon as I can find the time. But with the approach of Carnival . . ."

His voice trailed off as the telephone rang. "Excuse me, please," he murmured, and went out into the front hall to answer it.

When he reappeared in the doorway a moment later, Henri's eyes were closed and his face was white.

"Henri!" Frank sprang up and hurried over to him, taking his elbow. "Are you all right? Come sit down."

Henri dropped into his chair and held his hand over his eyes for a moment. Then he straightened up and said, "That was the police. Their inspectors have been checking over what is left of Snake Junot's car."

"I take it they found something?" Frank guessed.

Henri nodded. "Yes. There is no doubt about it. The reason the car exploded is that there was a bomb wired to the engine. Snake Junot was murdered!"

Chapter Seven

JOE COULD HARDLY believe his ears. "Murdered? But why?"

"And by whom?" Frank added.

Henri rubbed his temples with his fingertips. "I do not have the answers to these questions," he said. "The police have started to investigate. But I must decide what I'm to do. I cannot take the chance that the authorities will fail or that their investigation will take too long. This crime must be solved quickly.

"Winter Carnival is just six weeks away," Henri continued. "The ice-racing championship is very important to Dussault Motors, to the Auto Federation, and to all of Quebec. If the cloud of an unsolved murder, the murder of a champion driver, is hanging over it . . ."

"Of course," Frank murmured. Joe understood the look that Frank gave him next, and he nodded his agreement instantly.

"Can we help with the investigation?" Frank offered. "You know we've had a lot of experience."

"No, no, that would be unthinkable," Henri said, straightening up in his chair. "Thank you for the offer, but I cannot accept. This criminal is ruthless. He has already caused one death. I cannot expose the sons of an old friend to such danger. Besides, I invited you here to have a vacation, not to solve a mystery."

"Solving mysteries *is* our favorite kind of vacation," Joe insisted, grinning at his brother. "And we do know how to take care of ourselves."

"We can't promise that we'll succeed, but we'll certainly try," Frank added.

Henri looked from Joe to Frank and back to Joe. "Very well," he said at last. "I accept your kind offer."

"Can you tell us anything about Junot that might give us a lead to his killer?" Frank asked Henri.

Henri shrugged. "I have known Junot for several years, but he was not a friend of mine. I believe he came from a small town on the

Gaspé Peninsula, at the mouth of the Saint Lawrence. About his conduct, what can I say? He was a very good driver and a very bad sportsman."

"Do you know if he had any enemies?" asked Joe.

"Hardly anyone that I know liked him, and many had reason to dislike him. But between disliking a man and setting a bomb to kill him, there is a great distance," Henri replied.

"We should talk to the people who were at the press conference yesterday," Frank said. "Can you tell us how to get in touch with them?"

"The reporters, no," Henri replied. "But who else was there? Pierre, of course. François, Brent Moore . . . You might be able to find them at the Federation garage. If not, Pierre will have their addresses and telephone numbers. You can count on his cooperation. I am sure he must be as concerned to have this crime cleared up as I am."

Joe tried to think whether there was someone they were overlooking. "How about that girl, Danielle?" he asked.

"Ah, yes, you may find her at the garage also," said Henri. "And Marguerite Laforet, the actress, is now making a film here in town."

"Dangerous Loves," Frank supplied. "Our friends can tell us where she is."

"We'd better get to work," Joe said, standing up. "We'll let you know what we discover."

The Hardys went out to the front hall. As they were putting on their parkas, Frank said, "I've been replaying what happened yesterday afternoon, before the explosion. Check me on this: Junot drove his car over to the movie set, then drove it back. When we got to the garage, his car was inside, being tuned and fueled up, and he was outside, talking to the reporters. Right so far?"

Joe thought for a moment, then said, "Sounds good to me."

"So it looks as if the bomb must have been planted between the time he came back from the movie set and the time he set off on the publicity run," Frank continued.

"Right. And we can guess where, too," Joe added. "Inside the garage. Wiring a bomb to somebody's engine isn't the kind of thing you'd want anyone to see you doing."

"Good point," Frank said, opening the front door. "So we need to find out who went inside the garage while Junot's car was there. Come on, let's get over there."

The first thing the Hardys noticed when they pulled their rental car up to the boat house was a bright pink race car being wheeled out onto the ice.

"I'll bet that's Danielle's car," Frank said. "It's the same shade of pink as the racing coveralls she was wearing yesterday."

Joe scanned the area in front of the building for her. "I wonder—" he began, turning to Frank. "You remember that jealous scene she threw yesterday, just before Junot went off on his last run? Could she have been mad enough to want to kill him?"

"Maybe," Frank replied, frowning. "But people don't walk around with car bombs in their pockets. Junot's murder had to be planned in advance."

"Maybe she was mad at him for long enough to plan the bombing," Joe speculated. "Anyway, she can probably tell us more about Junot than anybody else. Let's see if she's inside."

One side of the boat house had been partitioned into offices. The first doorway had Pierre Desmoulins's name printed on the door. As the Hardys approached it, Joe could see Danielle through the open doorway. She was perched on the edge of Pierre's desk, wearing a black jumpsuit with pink stripes down the sides. Pierre was in his desk chair. The little office had only a desk, computer, and some shelves with papers and files on them.

"Ah, Frank, Joe," Pierre said as the Hardys

entered his office. "Come in. Danielle, these are friends of Monsieur Dussault, from the United States."

Danielle gave them a smile. "Weren't you here yesterday?" she asked. "I think I saw you just before—just before—" Her smile vanished, and she lowered her head to stare at the floor.

"There, there," Pierre said, taking her hand and patting it. "Danielle has had a terrible shock," he explained to Frank and Joe. "Two shocks, in fact. We learned this morning that the accident yesterday was not an accident at all."

"Yes, we heard," Frank said. "Please accept our sympathy. But that's really what we wanted to talk about. Henri Dussault has asked us to try to find out what happened. Would you mind if we ask you a few questions?"

Danielle looked at him. "About André, you mean?" She glanced over at Pierre. "I don't know, that's very—personal."

"I have some errands to do," Pierre said quickly. "Maybe you would like to use my office while I'm gone?" He turned on his answering machine and turned off his computer, then left.

"Do you mind telling us how long you and André Junot were, er, friends?" Frank asked.

Danielle made a sweeping gesture with her arm. "Since the very first time we met," she declared. "At last year's Winter Carnival. We saw each other, and it was the *coup de foudre,* the thunderbolt. But we could not let anyone else know."

Frank raised an eyebrow. "Why not?"

She gave her answer to Joe. "I am just beginning my career in racing," she said. "And André is—was a champion. I want people to respect me for my skill as a driver, not because of the people I am friendly with.

"You understand, don't you?" she added softly, touching Joe's arm. "It is a question of my pride."

"Sure, I understand," Joe said, his smile widening.

"I knew you would," Danielle continued. "When I saw your face, I said to myself, This is someone who is *symps.* That means sympathetic. Nice."

Oh, brother, thought Frank. Joe was eating up everything Danielle said, but Frank wasn't sure he bought her act. Why was she coming on to Joe like this?

"Danielle?" Frank said. "Yesterday, before the accident, did you notice anybody near André's car, anybody who shouldn't have been?"

"No," she said slowly. "The inspectors asked me this already today. There were all those reporters, all the photographers. I noticed only that André had his arms around another woman. I didn't realize who she was, that it was for publicity. Why was I so impetuous? The last words I spoke to him, I spoke in anger. I'll never forgive myself!"

She stood up and hid her face in her hands, then suddenly whirled around and began sobbing against Joe's shoulder. Joe was all too eager to put his arms around her.

"Then you didn't see anyone suspicious when you were inside the garage?" Frank quietly asked Danielle after a while.

He could see her body stiffen in Joe's arms. "Who told you I was inside the garage?" Danielle demanded, turning to glare at Frank.

"Weren't you? I thought I saw you come out of there," Frank continued. Why was she so defensive?

After a slight hesitation, Danielle said, "I was in the office. Perhaps I came out through the garage, I don't remember, but I saw nothing suspicious. Oh—I can't bear to think of yesterday!" She buried her face against Joe's chest again.

After a few moments, Danielle pulled back. "I am sorry," she whispered, wiping her eyes.

"You must think I am a fool. All this is too much for me. I can't talk about it any more, not now." With that, she ran out of the door.

"Aw, poor kid," Joe said. "She's really broken up about this."

"She certainly knew where to turn for comfort," Frank said, rolling his eyes.

"Come on, this is serious," Joe protested. "She was really upset!"

Frank crossed his arms over his chest. "Joe, the front of your parka isn't even tearstained. It's completely dry."

"It's nylon, it dries fast," Joe said, shooting Frank a cold look. "Besides, she probably cried so much already that she doesn't have any tears left."

"Yeah, right," Frank said. "That must be it. Face it, Joe. She snowed you."

"All right, all right," Joe said, holding up his hands. "Maybe you're right. Maybe. She might open up more if she wasn't talking to someone who's a detective." He snapped his fingers. "I know—what about Bess?"

"Good idea," said Frank. "Danielle seems pretty ambitious. Bess could say she's a reporter, planning to do a story about her."

Frank looked around as Pierre came into the office. "Sorry," Frank said. "We didn't mean to hog your office."

"Quite all right," the Auto Federation official replied. "Please tell me if there is any help I can give you. We must find out who committed this horrible crime as soon as possible."

This was just the offer they needed. "Could you possibly make us a list of people who were here yesterday afternoon?" Frank asked. "With addresses and telephone numbers, if you have them."

Pierre made a note on a pad on his desk. "Of course. Anything else?"

"Do you know where we can find François Volnay?" asked Joe.

Pierre raised both eyebrows but didn't comment. "Normally, François would be at Dussault Motors," he replied, "or working on that film. But it so happens that I saw him a few minutes ago in the garage here."

"Thanks," Frank said. "We'll see you later."

They found François talking to Brent Moore, the race car driver they had met the day before. The two were in the garage, studying what looked like parts of a carburetor.

"Hi," Joe called out. "Remember us? Joe and Frank Hardy. We're visiting Henri Dussault."

"Of course," François replied.

"We were wondering if you could spare a couple of minutes to talk," Frank asked.

Brent Moore scratched his bearded chin, then glanced at his watch. "I have to make an important call right now," he told them. "I'll be back."

As Brent walked away, François Volnay said, "A couple of minutes only."

"We know that you used to be the ice-racing champion of Quebec," Joe began.

" 'Used to be,' " François repeated bitterly. "And would be still, if there were justice in this world."

Frank could see that this was a touchy subject. "What happened?" he asked gently. "An accident, wasn't it?"

"A wreck, yes," François answered. "But you must not think that all wrecks are accidents."

Frank studied him closely. Was the ex-champion speaking of his own wreck or of the one that had killed Junot?

"Many people have had suspicions," François continued, "but I never spoke about it. The crash that left me with this stiff leg and ended my driving career was no accident. I was deliberately forced off the course—by Snake Junot."

"That's terrible," Joe said sympathetically. "But why did you keep it a secret? And why are you telling us now?"

"It was a matter of dignity. I do not make excuses," the former racer replied. "But now that Snake is dead, I do not wish people to remember him as a hero."

Joe was thinking that it was awfully convenient that no one could deny François's story now that Junot was dead.

"We're curious about what took place in the garage yesterday afternoon, while the mechanics were refueling Junot's car," Frank said. "Did you notice anything unusual?"

François became suspicious. "Why do you ask?"

"Henri Dussault is very concerned about the negative publicity that could result from the accident. He asked us to find out what we could about the accident," Joe explained.

"You might have noticed something that would explain what happened to Junot's car," Frank added.

"I noticed his new supercharger," François said. "A very effective and very expensive piece of equipment that will help his car go faster than ever."

Frank gave his brother a significant look. So Volnay *had* been in the garage when Junot's car was there.

"Nothing else?" Joe asked.

François snorted. "I have told all this to the

flics, the police," he said. "I saw no one put a bomb in Snake's car. Is that all?"

Frank suddenly remembered his promise to Nancy to question Volnay about the accidents on the movie set.

"I think so," Frank answered. Then, as if he'd only just thought of it, he said, "Hey, you're a technical advisor to *Dangerous Loves,* aren't you?" When Volnay nodded, Frank added, "They've had more than their share of accidents during the filming."

"It's true," François replied. "Their luck is very bad."

Brent reappeared in the garage in time to hear this. He rapped his knuckles on the wooden workbench and said, "Don't say things like that! I've just agreed to do some stunt driving in the movie."

"Yes?" said François. "Well, do not worry. Perhaps it was Snake who brought them bad luck. Now that he is gone . . ."

Frank tried to think of something to say that would elicit more information from François. "Do you plan to go on working in film after this?" he asked François.

"How many films are made in Canada that need my knowledge?" François replied bitterly. "When this one is finished, I go back to living on Henri Dussault's charity." Without another word, François Volnay limped out of the garage.

"Don't take it personally," Brent told Frank and Joe. "François was a great driver, a real champion. It was so hard when he was forced to give all that up."

Frank thought of something new then—the scene Danielle had made with Junot just before his fatal drive. She had accused him of flirting with Marguerite Laforet. It was a long shot, but maybe the romantic triangle would have some bearing on the case.

"You knew Junot fairly well," Frank said. "Did you have any reason to think that he might be seeing Marguerite Laforet, the movie star?"

The set of Brent's jaw hardened, and anger flashed out of his hazel eyes. "Who's been spreading mud like that?"

"No one," Frank told him. "I was just thinking about the way Danielle Rocheville carried on at the press conference—"

Brent sliced his hand through the air. "That was simply publicity. There was nothing between Junot and Marguerite Laforet—nothing at all!"

Joe seemed as taken aback by Brent's reaction as Frank was. "I didn't mean—" Frank started to say.

Brent took a step forward and jabbed his finger at Frank's face. "I don't care whose friends you are," he said through gritted teeth. "You stay away from me, and stay away from Miss Laforet, too. If you don't, you'll be very, very sorry. That's a promise!"

Chapter Eight

JOE WATCHED IN SURPRISE as Brent Moore strode out of the garage. Moments later he and Frank heard the roar of an engine. A spray of gravel from spinning tires hit the side of the building.

"We're getting pretty good at chasing away the people we want to question, aren't we?" Frank said with a wry smile.

Joe shook his head. "What was that all about?" he asked.

"Beats me," Frank replied. "But we've learned one thing—no, make that two. Both François Volnay and Brent Moore have quick tempers. And we already knew that both of them disliked Junot and wanted him out of the way."

"They both know enough about car engines to have planted that bomb," Joe added. "And they were both there yesterday."

"But how can we find out the truth from those two if they keep running away?" Frank asked.

"We know where to find them, anyway," Joe pointed out. "They're both working on *Dangerous Loves.* Maybe we should go have a talk with Nancy and Bess."

"Places, please. Places!"

The preparations for the morning's filming had taken over two hours, but at last everyone and everything was ready.

"Action!"

The tall, intricately carved door of Notre Dame Basilica swung open. Dennis, in his racing overalls, and Marguerite, in her floor-length white wedding dress, came out and started running down the steps. As they ran, they gazed at each other, laughing.

One of the cameras followed them down the steps while another, on the sidewalk, slowly backed away. As the two actors reached Dennis's red race car at the curb, Dennis picked Marguerite up in his arms and helped her through the window opening into the front seat.

"Cut!" shouted David.

A moment later Nancy saw what the problem was. Marguerite's dress had gotten caught on a piece of trim. A wardrobe person rushed forward and carefully disentangled it, then Dennis helped Marguerite out of the car again.

"I don't know if you should be laughing," the director said, stepping over to the couple.

Dennis brushed his black hair back from his face. "But you told us—" he started to say.

"I know, I know," David said, holding up his hand. "But it doesn't work. This is drama, not farce. Dennis, you should be determined, with just a hint of triumph. Marguerite, you are thrilled to be escaping with Dennis, but you are also frightened by your own daring. And for heaven's sake, keep that dress from getting caught again!"

The two actors started back up to the door of the church, and the camera crews returned to their original positions.

Just then Emily came over to join Nancy and Bess. "Have either of you seen Jack?" she asked worriedly. "He should have been here over an hour ago."

"Nope, sorry," Nancy replied. Bess shook her head.

"I don't understand it," Emily went on. "He knows we'll need stills of this scene for publicity. It's not like Jack to be irresponsible."

"He was supposed to have the contact sheets from yesterday's filming for me, too," Nancy said. "Did you talk to him this morning?"

Emily frowned. "No, I haven't seen or spoken to him since last night after our calèche ride. He was going to his friend Mike's studio to do the developing and printing. Maybe he fell asleep there," she added, her face brightening a little. "That must be it. I'll give him a call there."

Emily started toward the office trailer but was called over to a little group that included David Politano, Grant Shulman, and Billy Fitzgerald.

A few moments later Billy threw his arms in the air and stalked away. Emily hurried after him, talking earnestly. Billy shook his head with disgust, but Nancy noticed that at least he stopped to listen.

"Okay, ten-minute break," the woman with the bullhorn announced.

"It looks like another argument between David and Billy," Bess commented. "And poor Emily has gotten stuck with patching it up again."

Nancy nodded. "Hey," she said, thinking

out loud. "This might be a good time for me to ask Dennis about his hat."

"I'm coming, too," Bess announced firmly. "Just to make sure he gets fair treatment."

"And to get a look at those intense blue eyes," Nancy added, grinning at her friend.

They found the star just inside the doors of the basilica. "I noticed you weren't wearing your Stetson this morning, Dennis," Nancy said.

Dennis gave her a puzzled look. "It's funny you should say that," he said. "The fact is, I don't know where it is. I remember leaving it in the wardrobe trailer yesterday afternoon, but when I checked this morning, it wasn't there."

Nancy studied Dennis's face. He certainly didn't seem nervous. On the other hand, he *was* a trained actor, with years of practice at keeping his emotions from showing.

"Is this yours?" Nancy asked, lifting the cowboy hat out of the shopping bag.

Dennis's face lit up. "It sure is. But what are *you* doing with it?"

"We found it lying in the street last night," Nancy explained. "Right after somebody tossed a firecracker and spooked the horse that was pulling our calèche."

Nancy saw Dennis's jaw tighten as her words

sank in. "Now, hold on," he said. "I don't much like what you're implying. I have no idea what my hat was doing there, if it really was. And I certainly didn't throw any firecrackers at you. I've never liked practical jokes."

"I'm not sure it was a joke," Nancy told Dennis. "I think it was one more in the series of so-called accidents that's threatening this production."

After a slight pause, Dennis said, "Maybe you're right. But what does that have to do with me?"

Nancy decided to be honest. "Somebody mentioned that you wanted to get out of doing this film," she said. "Something about a part in a Hollywood feature that you had to turn down."

"There's no place like a movie company for gossip, is there?" Dennis said, his intense blue eyes flashing. "The more malicious, the better."

"But if *Dangerous Loves* is canceled, you won't be too upset, will you?" Nancy pressed.

Under the makeup, Dennis's face turned a dull red. "That's a filthy thing to say," he snapped.

"Dennis is right," Bess proclaimed. "If he did throw that firecracker, he would never have left his hat at the scene. Somebody was obviously trying to get him into trouble."

Nancy shot Bess a warning look. This was no time for her to let her crush on Dennis get in the way of their investigation.

"Why, thank you, Bess," Dennis said. "And I can't tell you what a treat it is to meet somebody who's so perceptive and understanding."

Nancy could practically see Bess's heart pounding through her jacket as the actor gave her a huge smile.

Just then a young man carrying a walkie-talkie came in the door and said, "We're starting, Dennis."

"Thanks, Paul," Dennis replied. Turning back to Bess, he smiled and asked, "Are you free for dinner tonight? I'd really like to get to know you better."

Bess's mouth fell open. "Why, yes," she finally managed to say. "Yes, of course!"

"Eight o'clock, at the Frontenac?" When Bess nodded, he said, "I'll see you then."

"Just promise me that you'll be sure to stay in public places," Nancy said when he'd left. "Dennis could be behind some pretty dangerous pranks. Come on, let's go over to the wardrobe trailer. Maybe somebody saw who took Dennis's hat—if he really did leave it there."

The wardrobe mistress, a very small, wiry woman in her sixties, wouldn't even let Nancy finish her question. "Do you know how many costumes I have to keep track of?" she demanded in a heavy Quebeçois accent. "Come back another time, when I am not so busy."

"So you didn't notice—" Nancy began.

"No, no, no!" The woman made shooing motions with her hands, as if chasing a couple of stray cats from the room. "Please, I am very occupied!"

"Well, at least she didn't tell us that Dennis *didn't* leave his hat in the trailer," Bess remarked once they were outside.

"She didn't tell us anything at all," Nancy pointed out. "I'd hardly say that clears him."

"Oh, there's Emily," Bess said. Emily was talking to a tall, bearded guy with a camera bag on his shoulder. "She still looks pretty worried."

"Nancy, Bess," said Emily after the girls reached her. "This is Mike Adams, Jack's friend. He says that Jack isn't at the studio."

"He was there last night, working in the darkroom," Mike told Nancy and Bess. "But I didn't see him this morning when I went by to pick up my equipment."

Nancy frowned. "Were you expecting him to be there?" she asked.

"Not really," Mike replied. "I was supposed to meet him here, to give him a hand."

"This isn't like Jack," Emily said, biting her

lower lip. "I'm going to call the hotel. Mike, can you cover for him, just for the rest of today?" she called over her shoulder, running to the office trailer.

"Sure, Emily," Mike replied.

When Emily hurried back out of the trailer, she shook her head and said, "No answer. I'll talk to you later, okay? After this scene?"

"Hey, look. There's Joe and Frank," Bess said, waving.

The Hardys were a dozen yards away, talking to a guard who was keeping spectators back. A moment later Nancy and Bess joined them and convinced the guard to let Frank and Joe past the barrier.

"Aren't you glad you have friends in high places?" Nancy teased. "What brings you guys here?"

"Something pretty shocking," Frank told her. "The explosion that killed André Junot yesterday wasn't an accident. There was a bomb in his car."

Nancy's stomach turned over. "That's horrible!" she exclaimed. "Have the police found out who put it there?"

"Not yet," said Joe. "Henri Dussault asked us to investigate, and we'd like a little help from you, Bess." Nancy listened as they told Bess about their plan regarding André Junot's girlfriend, Danielle.

"You think she'll be less suspicious if I pretend to be a reporter?" Bess asked. "I'll be glad to ask her a few questions. When?"

"Can you come back with me now?" Joe asked.

"Well, unless Nancy needs me here—"

"Go ahead," Nancy said quickly. "I'll wait here until you come back."

"Great," Frank said. "Why don't we meet back here in an hour or so? That ought to give me enough time to go to Dussault Motors."

After Joe and Bess left, Nancy spoke with Frank. "A murder case," she said softly. "I'll bet this wasn't the kind of vacation you two were expecting. If I can help in any way—"

"Thanks, Nancy," Frank replied. "Don't worry, I intend to pick your brains every chance I get. As a matter of fact, I'd like you to keep an eye on Volnay and Brent Moore while they're here. Joe and I will watch them at the Federation headquarters."

"Sounds good," said Nancy. "Did you get a chance to talk to François about the sabotage yet?" she asked.

Frank nodded. "If he's responsible, he didn't let on." Checking his watch, he added, "I'm going over to Henri's office to see what else I can find out about anyone involved in this ice-racing event."

"See you when you get back," Nancy said.

As Frank jogged past the security guard and out of sight, she turned back to the basilica's entrance.

Dennis and Marguerite were coming down the church steps for the fourth or fifth time. Dennis swung her up gracefully into his arms, and put her in the front seat of the car.

"Cut!" David called. He sounded almost cheerful. "That's a wrap! Okay, boys and girls, lunchtime. We resume shooting at one-thirty."

The extras and some crew applauded as Dennis and Marguerite took a comic bow and went off to their trailers.

Nancy did a double-take when, just a couple of minutes later, Marguerite stole out of her trailer and hurried off down the street. That was the second time she'd seen the actress vanish from the set, Nancy realized. Where did she go? Did she have anything to do with the accidents on the set? The next time Marguerite left the set, Nancy decided to follow her.

Nancy's thoughts were interrupted when Emily rushed over to her. "I still can't find Jack," she said in a trembling voice. "There's no answer at his hotel room or the studio. I telephoned the hospitals and the police. I even called his mother, in L.A. Where could he be?"

Nancy was beginning to worry about him now, too. Putting her arm around Emily's shoulders, she told her friend, "He's probably all right. We'll track him down. Let's go back to the hotel and talk the manager into opening his room for us," she suggested.

Leading Emily outside the barriers surrounding the basilica, Nancy managed to flag down a taxi. Ten minutes later they were back at the Château Frontenac. The two girls found the manager and explained their problem. After a lot of arguing and pleading, he agreed to take them up to Jack's room.

He tapped on the door and waited, then tapped again. Finally he put his passkey into the lock and opened the door.

"What is this?" he exclaimed. "What is this!"

Nancy peered around him and gasped. "Oh, no!" Beside her Emily cried, "This is awful!"

Jack's desk chair was overturned, and the dresser drawers were on the floor, their contents scattered. The sheets and blankets had been torn from the bed and tossed into the corner. The bare mattress had a gaping slit in its side. Even the pillows had been ripped open. Feathers stirred in the draft from the open door.

The manager started across the room toward the telephone.

"I wouldn't touch that," Nancy warned him.

"The police will want to check it for fingerprints."

The manager stopped in his tracks. "Police?" he repeated. "Mademoiselle, we do not summon the police to deal with unruly guests. We simply make sure that they pay for all the damage they have done."

"I don't think we're talking about an unruly guest this time," Nancy cut in, stepping firmly up to the manager. "We have been unable to locate our friend all morning, and his room has been ransacked. I think we're dealing with a case of foul play!"

Chapter Nine

"I DON'T BELIEVE THIS," Emily said, and slumped wearily against the wall of the room.

As the manager left to call the police, Nancy put an arm around Emily's shoulders. The two girls waited silently until he returned.

"I am sorry, mademoiselle," a Sergeant Lagioule said to Emily after looking over the room ten minutes later. "There is nothing here to prove that your friend did not leave of his own accord. If he has not returned in a day or so, we will make further inquiries."

Emily stared at him in disbelief. "What about the way his room was left?" she demanded. "Just look at it! You mean to tell me that nothing is wrong?"

"Not at all," the police officer replied. "If you want my personal opinion, this does not look one bit good. But I am bound by regulations and department policy. People have a right to go away without informing their friends of their plans."

"That's the most ridiculous—" Emily started to say.

"Let it go, Emily," said Nancy. She sensed that any more protests would be useless. "If Jack doesn't turn up by tomorrow, we'll be in touch with you again."

Emily bristled as Sergeant Lagioule left the room. "What do you mean, let it go?" Emily demanded.

"The police may not be able to do anything yet," Nancy hurried to explain. "But there's nothing to stop us from investigating."

The manager was hovering near the door. "I'm sorry, you'll have to leave now," he said. "I must lock this room."

"Of course," Nancy said at once. Then, "Oh, rats," she added. "I must have dropped my pen. I have to find it. My father gave it to me, and it's very valuable."

The hotel official clearly didn't like the idea of letting Nancy and Emily search the room, but Nancy insisted.

"Look for anything that seems out of place and anything that should be here but isn't," Nancy whispered to Emily.

Nancy started near the closet, while Emily checked through the clothes scattered on the floor.

"Ladies, I really must insist," the manager spoke up from the doorway five minutes later. He was tapping his foot impatiently.

Nancy smiled at him and said sweetly, "I just want to try one more spot." She leaned over to peer behind the dresser.

What was that? Getting down on her hands and knees, she groped in the narrow space between the dresser and wall. A moment later she grabbed something and slid it into the pocket of her skirt. Standing up, she went over to Emily and asked in a low voice, "Jack doesn't smoke, does he?"

"No," Emily answered. "Why?"

With a glance at the manager, Nancy just said, "I'll tell you outside."

"Ladies, I apologize, but—" the hotel official began again.

"It's all right, we're just leaving," Nancy said quickly. "Thanks for being so helpful."

Downstairs, Emily said excitedly, "You found something, didn't you?"

Nancy pulled a small, flat matchbox from

her pocket. "This was behind the dresser. It's from the Auberge des Remparts."

"Nancy!" Emily exclaimed. "That's the hotel where Billy is staying."

"Of course, anyone could have dropped those matches. But they could mean that Billy had something to do with Jack's disappearance."

"Why would he want to hurt Jack?" Emily asked. A tear ran down her cheek. "Why would anyone hurt him? Everybody likes Jack."

"We don't know that anybody hurt him," Nancy pointed out. "Maybe he disappeared on purpose, because he knew somebody was after him."

"But who? Why? It doesn't make sense," Emily insisted.

Nancy's brows furrowed into a V as she tried to put together the pieces of the puzzle. "Somebody must have been searching for something Jack had," Nancy began. "They pulled out all the drawers and slit open the mattress."

"I don't see what he could have that would be so important," Emily said.

"Jack's a photographer," Nancy went on. "The most likely possibility is a photo—one that's dangerous to somebody."

Emily stared at Nancy with fear in her

brown eyes. "They wouldn't hurt him, would they?"

"I don't know," Nancy said simply. "The best thing we can do, for Jack's sake, is to clear up this mystery as quickly as possible."

Nancy started for the door. "I'm going to try to talk to some of the housekeeping staff. Maybe someone saw something. Then I'm going to ask Mike to let me take a look around his studio and darkroom."

She smiled at Emily. "Don't worry. I'm sure we'll turn up some clue as to what happened to Jack."

"That's Danielle's car," Joe said in an undertone as he pulled into the lot by the Auto Federation's temporary headquarters. He pointed to the pink racer across the lot. "She must be inside."

"I feel shaky," Bess admitted. "Are you sure she'll talk to me?"

Joe smiled. "I'm going to tell her that you're a reporter from the U.S., doing a story about ice racing. After what happened, you want to write a feature about her and Snake Junot."

"Isn't that a little, well, ghoulish?" Bess protested. "I mean, after all, it was just one day ago that her boyfriend's car blew up."

"Reporters do that kind of thing all the

time," said Joe. "Anyway, Danielle seems to like attention."

They found Danielle in the garage, chatting with Brent Moore. When Brent saw Joe, he stalked out of the room. Obviously, Brent was still angry at him and Frank for asking about Junot's romantic involvements with Danielle and Marguerite.

"Joe," Danielle said breathily. "I was wondering when I would see you again." Then she noticed Bess for the first time. "You have brought a little friend. How nice," she said in a tone that clearly conveyed her displeasure.

Joe introduced Bess and explained what she wanted. Danielle swallowed the cover story at once. "It is a true tragedy," she told Bess.

"For now I'll just ask some easy questions," Bess said. "How did you and Mr. Junot first meet?"

Danielle launched into an account of their meeting at the ice race the year before and how much André had taught her at her first big race.

"Just last week," Danielle continued, "André had a small birthday party. Just a few friends and the press. I made him his favorite chocolate cake. It is the first time I made a cake, and I was sure it would be a disaster. But André told me that it was the best he ever ate. I think maybe he was telling a little untruth."

Bess smiled. "I'm sure he must have appreciated it very much. But there's another side to this story—a tragic side, isn't there? Can you think of anybody who might have been his enemy?"

"All great men, all champions, have enemies," Danielle said with a sigh. "André, too."

"Anyone in particular?" Bess asked. "The story will be much more dramatic if I can work up the tension between him and someone else."

Joe silently cheered Bess. She was doing a great job of pressing Danielle for information.

"I will not mention names," Danielle replied. "Look among those he beat to become champion." She seemed to have become uncomfortable with Bess's questions. "I have nothing more to say about this."

"Do you have any photos of the two of you?" Bess asked.

Danielle pulled a handkerchief from the pocket of her jumpsuit and turned away. "I have only my memories," she said in a muffled voice. "Please, I cannot bear to talk about it anymore."

Joe met Bess's eyes and motioned with his head toward the door.

"I understand, Danielle," Bess said gently. "I hope we can talk again soon. And please accept my sympathy."

Outside, Bess turned to Joe. "Was I okay?" she asked.

"You were terrific," Joe replied, grinning at her. "I was hoping she'd say more about Junot's enemies, but you did your best."

"There's one thing that surprised me a little," Bess said slowly, giving Joe a probing look. "The way she acted toward you when we first walked in."

"What do you mean?" Joe asked.

Bess shook her head. "Danielle was definitely flirting with you, and that just doesn't seem to fit with what she was telling me. I don't trust her, Joe."

"Because she likes me?" Joe countered. "What's wrong with that?"

Bess rolled her eyes at him. "You're hopeless, Joe Hardy!"

Frank stared at the Dussault Motors building, where the taxi had let him off. It was a four-story warehouse-type building, in an industrial section of the Lower Town. After going inside, Frank asked for Henri.

As he entered Henri's office, Frank noticed a big window behind his friend's desk that overlooked the main work floor. Teams of mechanics were swarming over half a dozen sleek, brightly painted cars.

"Beautiful, aren't they?" Henri said, following Frank's gaze. "But you did not come here just to admire my cars.

"As I said on the telephone," Henri went on, "you are welcome to look through my files on the Winter Carnival ice racing. I also have access to the records of the Auto Federation, although I am not sure what you would hope to find in them."

"I'm not sure, either," Frank confessed. "But Junot's death probably had something to do with his career. Where are the files, by the way?"

Henri gestured to a gray filing cabinet. "Those are mine." Then he pointed to the computer terminal in a corner. "The Auto Federation office is in Montreal, so we have a telephone to the Auto Federation system. It saves the organization the expense of setting up a separate system here in Quebec, just for the ice-racing season."

"But isn't it inconvenient for the Federation officials to come down here to access their computer files?" Frank asked.

"Pierre's office computer, down at the boat house, is networked with our system. He can store and recover information there."

Henri led Frank over to the terminal and showed him how to access the Auto Federation's files. "If you need to make a hard copy of anything," Henri added, "just hit the Print

Screen button. The printer is in the closet behind you. I cannot stand the noise it makes."

Frank was scanning through the list of files when he heard Henri say, "Oh, François! I thought you were working on the film today."

François Volnay nodded coolly to Frank, then told Henri, "This afternoon, they are filming inside the basilica, so they don't need me. I thought I would use the time to catch up on my work here."

"Fine, fine," said Henri, clapping François on the back. "Let's go downstairs and leave my young friend to his investigation."

Turning his attention to the computer screen, Frank began pulling up files, scanning for anything that seemed unusual or out of place. He even read the minutes of the most recent Auto Federation directors' meeting. A reference to the prize fund for the ice-racing event aroused his curiosity.

Frank checked the directory for a Prize Fund listing. Pulling it up, he saw that it was a chronological statement of the status of the prize fund account at a bank in Quebec.

A deposit of half a million Canadian dollars had been made to the account three months earlier. Frank's gaze slid down the figures. The account didn't show any change until—

Frank sat bolt upright in his chair. What was

this? He grabbed a pencil and scribbled some figures on a pad, then stared at the result.

There was no question about it. In the last two weeks large sums of money had been moved out of the prize fund account. There might be some legitimate reason for it. But if not, it looked as if someone was stealing money from the Federation—*lots* of money!

Chapter Ten

I'VE GOT TO show this to Henri," Frank said aloud, still staring at the print screen.

He quickly hit the Print Screen button, then jumped up and went over to the closet, waiting while the printer noisily tapped out the figures. After tearing off the sheet of paper, he went in search of Henri.

Frank found him down in the main workroom and showed him the printout of the prize fund account.

"Quelle horreur!" Henri exclaimed under his breath. Frank wasn't positive what it meant, but he was willing to bet it wasn't good. "We'd

better go back to my office," Henri added gravely.

Once there, Henri paced back and forth in front of the desk. "I do not believe this," he said. "Who would do such a thing? And how? In order to make a computer withdrawal, it is necessary to know the password to the prize fund account. I chose the password myself, and I have not shared it with anyone."

"Someone must have figured it out," said Frank, sitting down in front of the computer again. "Until about two months ago, there weren't any withdrawals from the account. Then, in late October, somebody withdrew five dollars. Why so little? Unless they were testing their password."

Henri nodded, studying the printout with fresh interest. "Then, nothing more until three weeks ago," Henri said. "So why did they suddenly start taking out two thousand dollars a week? To my mind, such a sum is too large to be overlooked but not large enough to justify the risk."

Frank studied the piece of paper with Henri. "I don't know," he said. "Maybe they're regular payments for something.

"That's odd," he added, pointing to the bottom of the printout. "There was no two-thousand-dollar withdrawal this week."

"Yes, it is odd," Henri said. "There is something else I do not understand. How could the embezzler have hoped to avoid being found out?"

Frank thought for a moment. "How often do you check on this account?" he asked Henri.

"Not often," Henri admitted. "Why should I? The prize fund sits in the account until Winter Carnival, when the money is withdrawn. If I check it at all, I just glance at the monthly statement from the bank. And to my knowledge, no one else even bothers with the statement."

"The crook must have gambled on that. He figured he'd have four or five weeks before anyone would notice anything."

"This is very bad," said Henri. "If word of this embezzlement gets out, the Auto Federation and Dussault Motors could be involved in a tremendous scandal. And just before our most important event of the season! Frank, if you and Joe can get to the bottom of this—"

"We'll do our best," Frank promised. "I don't think you should tell anyone about this yet. You ought to change the password on that account right away, though."

Frank spent the next half hour going through the remainder of the Auto Federation computer files and Henri's files. He didn't see anything that shed further light on the embezzlement or on Junot's murder. Saying goodbye to Henri, he headed down the hallway toward the stairway.

He didn't know if the stolen money had anything to do with Junot's murder, but he was definitely going to find out.

Out of the corner of his eye Frank saw François Volnay ducking into the stairway, a briefcase in his hand. He shot a nervous glance at Frank before disappearing down the stairs. Frank got to the outside entrance just in time to see Volnay get into his car and drive away.

"Weird," Frank murmured aloud, staring after the car. Volnay had told Henri that he was going to spend the afternoon catching up on his work at Dussault Motors. So why was he suddenly taking off?

By the time Frank got a taxi, François Volnay's car was well out of sight.

As he rode back to the basilica, Frank started making a mental list of suspects. *If* there was a connection between the embezzlement scheme and Junot's murder, the culprit had to be somebody who was familiar with Auto Federation *and* someone who had been at the Federation garage before the publicity run. Plenty of people fit that description—Brent and Danielle and Pierre, for starters. But at the top of Frank's list was François Volnay.

Frank checked his watch. Joe should be back

at the movie location by now. It would be interesting to hear what he and Bess found out from questioning Danielle. After that, he would examine François Volnay.

Mike's studio was in a former stable, behind an old house near the city walls. Nancy used the set of keys he had lent her to get in.

She entered what was apparently the main room of the studio. Enormous rolls of heavy paper in different colors were mounted on the far wall. Nancy guessed that they were used as backdrops.

She took a quick look around the room. There was a set of flat file drawers in one corner, but the photos inside weren't of the movie set. They were all probably Mike's.

Three doors led off the main room. The first went to a kitchenette. Behind the second door Nancy found a tiny bedroom with a bathroom attached. The third led to the darkroom.

Stepping inside, Nancy turned on the ceiling light. "Bingo!" she said out loud. On the counter next to the enlarger was a large metal file box, about a foot long on each side, with *Dangerous Loves* printed on the top in Magic Marker. She unlatched and lifted the lid. Jack was clearly methodical. Each of the thick file folders in the box was labeled with a date and scene numbers.

Her heart racing, Nancy reached for the last file and pulled it out. The date marked on the folder was two days earlier. Where was yesterday's file? she wondered, frowning. Had it been misplaced? She flipped through the folders, one by one, but there was no trace of one for December 27.

Nancy could think of three explanations. Jack hadn't gotten around to making up a file for that date, or he had taken the file with him, or it had been taken by the person who ransacked his hotel room.

No, there was another possible explanation as well. Maybe Jack hadn't gotten around to developing those rolls yet. Nancy let her gaze travel around the darkroom. Her eyes lit on a wastebasket.

Pulling the wastebasket out from under the sink, Nancy leafed through it. Near the top was a damp pile of test strips, small pieces of photographic paper that Jack had used to decide on the proper exposure for prints.

She peeled the strips apart and laid them out on the table. Some were too light or too dark to make out anything in them. But on one of the strips was part of a frame that included Bess's face. So Jack must have developed yesterday's film, and he had at least started to print contact sheets.

Another of the test strips caught Nancy's

eye. It was an enlargement and showed a man climbing into a race car. She caught her breath as she recognized André Junot's square face.

The photo must have been taken just before he set off on his fatal run, Nancy realized. Was there something special about the photograph that had made Jack take the time to enlarge it? The print was too light and hazy to make out any details.

Nancy found a manila envelope and tucked the test strips inside. Then she left the studio, being careful to lock the door behind her.

As she walked back to Notre Dame, Nancy went over the case. It was appearing more and more likely that the missing negatives contained evidence that could incriminate whoever was sabotaging *Dangerous Loves*.

If only she had more to go on! She couldn't help thinking that Billy was somehow involved. He hated David Politano, and the matches from his hotel had been found in Jack's ransacked room. Then there was Dennis. Nancy still wasn't convinced he hadn't set off the firecracker that had scared their horse, but she needed evidence.

When Nancy got back to the basilica, movie trailers were still lined up outside, but there were no crowds on the steps. She followed the bundles of black power cables through the front door of the church and found a complete wedding procession standing just inside. She had to admit the scene was impressive. If it hadn't been for the light stands and cameras, she would have thought she was interrupting a real wedding.

Filming was about to begin, so Nancy hurried farther inside the basilica and away from the wedding procession. Seeing Bess in an arched alcove, Nancy went over to join her.

"Did you find Jack?" Bess whispered anxiously. "Emily told me what happened. She's been crying all afternoon." She nodded at the other side of the basilica, where a very pale Emily was listening to something one of the sound people was saying.

"Jack wasn't there," Nancy told Bess, then quickly explained about the missing negatives. "Are Frank and Joe still here?" she asked.

Bess shook her head. "They had to leave. Frank said something about digging up dirt on some guy."

"Shhh!" somebody said.

Bess looked around apologetically. Then she turned back to Nancy. "Isn't it beautiful?" she whispered.

Nancy glanced around, taking in the basilica's interior. Except for the wooden pews, the church was all in white and gold. "It certainly is," Nancy whispered back.

"Not the church," Bess replied, giggling. "The procession. I just *adore* weddings!"

Grant Shulman hurried over then, the bright lights shining on his bald head. "Keep out of the way, please," the assistant director told Nancy and Bess. "Okay, bridal procession, take your places."

He grabbed a little boy with a scrubbed face and carefully combed brown hair, who was carrying two rings on a satin cushion, and tugged him to the front. A little girl in a white lace dress, with a ribbon-decked basket of roses on her arm, got in line behind him.

Bess frowned. "That's not right," she said to Nancy. She looked around. "Mr. Shulman," she called. "Oh, Mr. Shulman!"

"What is it?" the assistant director said. "I'm very busy."

"It's the procession," Bess told him. "You've got the order wrong. The flower girl goes first, *then* thc ring bearer."

"This is what's in the script," he said, and walked away.

"But I know it's wrong," Bess insisted.

"If you don't keep out of my way and stop interfering, I'll have you thrown off the set!"

"What a grouch," Bess said huffily. "I *am* right, you know," she told Nancy.

Nancy wasn't really paying attention. She

was busy scanning the crowd for Billy. He didn't seem to be there. Maybe David had sent him off to do more rewrites. Unless he was lurking nearby, arranging another "accident."

Just then Marguerite emerged from one of the curved archways across from where Nancy and Bess were standing. She went to the basilica's entrance, where David was checking the procession.

"Are we all ready?" he asked. "Father of the bride? Bridesmaids?" His glance fell on the ring bearer, then on the flower girl, who gave him a timid smile.

Suddenly David whirled around and said loudly, "Who set up the procession?"

There was a long silence before Grant stepped forward and mumbled, "I did."

"Don't you know anything about weddings?" David demanded. "The flower girl goes first!"

He turned to the little girl, who by now appeared terrified. Putting his hand on her shoulder, he nudged her forward, in front of the ring bearer.

"Come on now, sweetheart," he said. "No holding back. You're the one who leads the procession. That makes you the star of the show."

Nancy's gaze went back to Grant Shulman. The assistant director had stepped back into one of the archways and was staring at David with hatred in his eyes.

A moment later Nancy felt the hairs rise on the back of her neck. Grant still wore the same look of intense loathing—only now it was directed at her and Bess.

Chapter Eleven

"DON'T LOOK NOW, Bess, but I think we just made an enemy," Nancy said, poking her friend.

"Wow, Grant does look like he wants to kill us," she whispered. "But why?"

"He's probably the kind of person who just can't admit when he's wrong," Nancy said.

Bess didn't say anything. In fact, she didn't seem to have heard Nancy at all. Her attention was fixed on something near the rear corner of the basilica.

"Oh, look, there's Dennis," she said excitedly a moment later. "I've been meaning to tell him how great I thought his acting was this morning." Bess nervously checked out her sweater and slacks. "Do I look okay?"

For half a second Nancy thought of trying to warn her friend against Dennis again. But instead she smiled and said, "You look fantastic."

As Bess went over to the star, Nancy set her jaw. "I'd better find out about Dennis Conners," she murmured to herself, "before my best friend goes out to dinner with a guy who could be dangerous."

Nancy waited until the first take of the wedding procession had been shot, then slipped outside. In the late afternoon light she walked over to the costume trailer.

She found the diminutive, gray-haired wardrobe mistress sitting down, with a container of tea in her hand. Nancy was grateful that the woman didn't seem busy now.

"Hi." Nancy greeted her with a big smile. "I dropped by this morning, to ask about Dennis Conners's hat."

The woman nodded silently.

"Mr. Conners told me he left his hat here yesterday afternoon," Nancy went on. "Can you tell me if that's true?"

"I am responsible for costumes. Personal property is not my concern. If Monsieur

Conners left his hat here, that is his affair. And if he asked a friend to come and get it for him, that, too, is his affair."

"Is that what happened?" Nancy asked. "A friend picked it up?"

The small woman gave a grudging nod.

"Do you know who the friend was? His name? What he looked like?"

"I was too pressed to notice," the woman replied. "He was a Yankee, that is all I can tell you. Now, please, I am very busy."

Busy drinking her tea, Nancy thought as she left the trailer. At least she now had more information.

It was completely dark now. But as Nancy started up the steps to the basilica, she could make out Bess emerging from the ornate entrance.

"I didn't know where you'd gone," Bess said, meeting Nancy halfway down the steps. "They're nearly done filming in there, so I'm going back to the hotel. I want to get ready for tonight."

"Your big date with Dennis?" Nancy asked. "Listen, Bess—"

"Don't bother," Bess interrupted, holding up her hand. "I've already memorized the words *and* the tune. Yes, I'll be careful. No, I won't forget that Dennis is a suspect."

"That's what I wanted to tell you," Nancy

said, laughing. "I just talked to the wardrobe mistress, and she confirmed Dennis's story about his leaving his hat in the trailer. Someone *else* came and took it, an American. So, it looks to me as if Dennis is in the clear, Bess. You were right about him." She gave Bess a quick hug and added, "I really hope everything works out between you two."

"Thanks, Nan," Bess said with a grin. Looking at her watch, Bess exclaimed, "Oh my gosh, it's almost five. Dennis is picking me up at eight. I have only three hours to get ready for dinner! Are you coming, now?"

Nancy shook her head. "I'm staying here. I've noticed that when filming wraps, Marguerite always leaves in a real hurry. I want to find out where she goes. I'll see you later, and have a great time tonight, Bess."

As Bess took off down the street, Nancy reentered the basilica. The crew was gathered in one section of pews, and David was just saying, "That's all, folks. Get a good night's sleep."

Nancy quickly slipped back outside and hid behind a pillar. Moments later Marguerite came out, wearing a down coat over her wedding dress. She hurried to her trailer, with Nancy following at a distance.

In what seemed like an impossibly short time, Marguerite came out again. Pulling the hood of her down coat up around her face, she glanced furtively in both directions before darting off down the street. Nancy waited until the actress was a hundred feet ahead, then went after her.

The way Marguerite was behaving, it was obvious that she didn't want anyone to know where she was going.

Hardly anyone was out on the snowy, winding streets, which were illuminated only by an occasional street lamp. After five minutes Marguerite paused at a side street, glanced over her shoulders quickly, and dashed to the right. Nancy hurried after her and peered around the corner. The street was empty. Marguerite had vanished!

Frustrated, Nancy surveyed the block. All the shops along the street were closed and dark. About halfway down the narrow road, however, a pool of warm light spilled out from the windows of a restaurant.

Nancy was about to check it out when she saw a man with a cap pulled down low over his eyes moving toward her from the other direction. He stopped in front of the restaurant and checked both ways before going inside. A moment later two shadowy figures hurried up the dark street and slipped into a doorway, directly across the street from the restaurant.

Nancy ducked into a recessed doorway, hoping she hadn't been spotted. She had been tailing suspects long enough to know when someone was being followed. Those two people were definitely tailing the guy who'd just entered the restaurant.

Nancy finally decided that acting innocent would be the best tactic.

Pulling her scarf up close around her face, she walked up to the restaurant. Nancy glanced across the street, but she couldn't distinguish the figures in the doorway.

There was a menu posted in the restaurant window. She stopped in front of it and pretended to read it while she attempted to see inside. Her pulse began to race when she spotted Marguerite sitting at a table. She was with a man with short blond hair and a beard. Nancy didn't recognize the guy. She only knew he *wasn't* Jack.

Nancy was wondering if she should go inside when Marguerite glanced up and saw her. She said something to her companion, who immediately sprang up and headed for the door.

Nancy started to retreat, but someone grabbed her arms from behind.

Nancy's breath caught in her throat. The men in the doorway! Without thinking, she lifted her foot and brought it down hard on her assailant's foot.

"Ow!" said a familiar voice. "What did you do that for?"

"Joe!" Nancy exclaimed. "What are you doing here?"

Before he could answer, the restaurant door swung open and the blond-haired, bearded man came charging out, fists clenched. Behind him, Marguerite watched with round, frightened eyes.

"Take it easy, Brent," said Joe.

Brent? Nancy silently echoed. This guy must be Brent Moore, the stunt driver Emily hired to take André's place in *Dangerous Loves.*

"Why are you following us!" Brent growled. "Digging up dirt for your reporter friend? I'd like to flatten you!"

Seeing the way Joe glared back at the race car driver, Nancy quickly stepped between the two.

"What are you talking about? I made a date to meet my friends here for dinner," she fibbed. "Somebody told me it's great. Marguerite! Hi, I didn't see you."

Brent glanced from Nancy to Joe in confusion. Marguerite said, "I think there's been some mistake. Please excuse us." She took Brent's arm and led him back inside.

"Where's Frank?" Nancy asked.

"Here I am, playing backup," Frank replied. "Let's go eat for real. We're not going to have any luck tailing those two now that they're onto us."

The three detectives found a small restaurant a few blocks away and took a table in the corner so they could talk freely.

After they had gotten their appetizers, Nancy looked at Frank and Joe and said, "Now, would you guys mind telling me what was going on back there?"

"We went to the Auto Federation looking for François Volnay—he's our top suspect for Junot's murder," Joe explained. "He wasn't there, but Brent Moore was."

"He was Junot's biggest rival, *and* he was around the garage before the explosion," Frank added. "So we thought we should follow him. What about you?"

Nancy told the Hardys about Marguerite's mysterious departures from the set. "I thought she might have something to do with Jack's disappearance," she concluded. "But that doesn't seem very likely now."

"Why not?" said Joe. "Maybe Brent and Marguerite are in cahoots? Maybe Brent put the bomb in Junot's car and Marguerite created a diversion. Or maybe Brent is helping Marguerite sabotage *Dangerous Loves.*"

"I think there might be another possibility," Nancy said thoughtfully. "When I looked through that restaurant window, Marguerite and Brent didn't act like conspirators to me. They seemed to be lovers."

"But then why all the secrecy?" Frank said. "I think they definitely have something to hide."

"Speaking of being in love," Joe put in, "where's Bess?"

Nancy smiled. "She has a date with Dennis Conners," she replied.

"The lead in the movie?" Frank asked, frowning. "But I thought he was one of your suspects?"

"*Was* is the right word," Nancy told him as their main courses arrived. "I found out that someone else took his hat from the wardrobe trailer yesterday, so Dennis is in the clear—about the firecracker incident, anyway."

"I'm stuffed!" Nancy announced as they left the restaurant. "I think that was the most delicious steak and fries I've ever had."

Joe nodded his agreement. "That custard thing, the crème caramel, was great, too."

Frank linked arms with Nancy, while Joe took her other arm. "We'll walk you back to the Frontenac," Frank insisted.

Light snow was falling, and it glistened under the street lamps as they made their way down the narrow, winding streets. Some of the houses were decorated with strings of colored Christmas lights and blinking replicas of the Carnival snowman.

"I love being in a city where you can walk almost everywhere," Nancy said as they turned onto a narrow street that led to the Château Frontenac.

She jumped as headlights suddenly flared behind them and a powerful engine was gunned.

Frank shouted, "Look out! Jump!"

Nancy glanced back and saw a car speeding down the center of the narrow street, heading straight at them!

There wasn't a second to think. Seeing a low cast-iron fence to her right, Nancy dived head-first over it. Her shoulder hit the pavement, and she tucked into a ball.

Breathing deeply, she raised her head just as a dark-colored sports car sped past, its right wheels on the sidewalk. If she had moved any more slowly, the car would have hit her for sure.

Before Nancy could get a look at the license plate, the sports car had reached the end of the block and turned and vanished.

"You okay?" she heard Frank and Joe call from across the street.

Nancy stood up and dusted off her parka

and jeans skirt. "I'm going to be black and blue tomorrow," she reported with a shaky smile, "but nothing serious."

"I ripped my down parka on the fence," said Joe. "And I just bought it for this trip. If I get my hands on that crazy driver—"

"Crazy?" Frank repeated skeptically. "I think he knew what he was doing."

"Did you see who it was?" Nancy asked.

Frank shook his head. "No, but *someone* followed us," Frank pointed out. "There's been one death already, and the murderer might be ready to kill again—to protect his identity. We may not think we're close to solving the case, but *he* might. From now on, I think we all better be careful about taking evening strolls down lonely alleys."

"Dennis is a fantastic dancer," Bess told Nancy the next morning. They were still in their nightgowns and bathrobes, eating an early breakfast of brioches and café au lait at the table in their hotel room.

"The club we went to was really hot. I was starting to think that Quebec was a little staid—you know, beautiful but not too exciting. After last night, I've definitely changed my mind. Everyone was going crazy on the dance floor.

"Speaking of which," she went on, "have

you started thinking about a costume for the New Year's Eve party?"

Nancy blinked in surprise. "I forgot all about it."

"Nancy! It's going to be sensational, and it's only two days away. I can't wait."

Nancy answered a knock at the door and found Emily standing there, her eyes red and puffy.

"I'm not going to wait any longer," she announced. "I'm going to the police this morning, before I have to be on location. Will one of you come with me?"

Nancy glanced at Bess and asked, "How fast can you get dressed?"

Ten minutes later all three girls were outside in a taxi. After a short ride, they were at police headquarters, in the office of Sergeant Lagioule.

"There's been no sign of my friend for over twenty-four hours," Emily said.

The sergeant sighed and pulled out a form. "Fill this out as completely as possible, please," he said. "Do you have a photo of your friend?"

Emily pulled one from her wallet and passed it over.

"Do you think you'll find him?" Emily asked when she finished.

"We'll do all we can, mademoiselle," the police officer said. "People very seldom disappear for long—unless, of course, they want to."

He stood up and showed them out of his office. At the door he added, "I will see that you are kept informed of our progress, mademoiselle."

"Thank you, Sergeant," Emily replied. She was silent until they were partway down the block. Then she said, "It's hopeless. They're not going to do a thing. They don't even believe anything's wrong!"

"Then we'll just have to find Jack ourselves," Nancy said.

This was the first chance she'd had to speak to Emily since they'd discovered Jack's ransacked room the morning before. Nancy quickly filled her in on what she found when she'd visited Jack's studio.

"Will Mike be shooting stills for *Dangerous Loves* again today?" she asked Emily. "I want to ask him about the test strips."

"He should be," Emily replied. "I asked him to fill in as long as—as long as Jack's away."

They walked to the broad, snow-covered park where they'd be shooting that day. Nancy was surprised by the dozens of snow sculptures glistening in the sunlight.

"Look at that huge snow castle over there," cried Bess.

"The snow sculpture contest is one of the biggest events of Winter Carnival," Emily explained with a wan smile. "Of course, we had to have these built for the film. They did a good job, but I hear the real sculptures are even more spectacular."

Emily went to the office trailer to check on arrangements for the day's shoot. And Bess went to chat with Dennis.

Finding herself alone, Nancy scanned the park for Billy Fitzgerald. It was odd—she hadn't seen him since she found that matchbook from his hotel. It could just be a coincidence, or it could mean he had something to do with Jack's disappearance.

Nancy did spot Mike Adams, though. He was standing near a huge snow dragon.

"Hi," he said when Nancy walked up to him. "I still haven't heard a word from Jack. Did you learn anything at the studio yesterday?"

"I think so," Nancy replied. She handed him the spare set of keys he'd lent her, along with the envelope of test strips she found in the darkroom.

"I know Jack made these the night before last," she said. "Look at this." She pointed to the hazy print of the photo of Junot in his race car. "Do you have any idea why he'd enlarge this photo?"

"Wait a minute," Mike said, snapping his fingers. "That's right! Jack told me he was going to print some of those up. He had a date to show them to the head honcho at the Auto Federation. He said he was hoping to wangle an assignment from the Federation to cover the Winter Carnival ice racing."

"*When* was he planning to talk to the Auto Federation?" Nancy asked.

Mike thought for a moment before answering. "Jack told me he'd made an appointment with the guy for yesterday morning. He wanted to be done in plenty of time to get to Notre Dame before the shooting started."

"He never arrived at the basilica, and he's been missing ever since," Nancy pointed out. "I wonder if he kept that appointment. If he did, whoever he met probably was the last person to see Jack before he vanished!"

Chapter Twelve

"THANKS FOR THE INFO," Nancy said, taking the test strips back from Mike. "I'll see you later."

Nancy hurried to the office trailer. Emily looked up when Nancy came in.

"May I use the telephone?" Nancy asked. She pulled from her purse the paper Frank had given her with Henri's telephone number. "I think I may have a lead."

Emily's face lit up. "Really? What is it? The phone's right there," she said in a rush.

Nancy explained while she dialed Mr. Dussault's number. A woman answered in

French but said, "One moment," when Nancy asked for Frank or Joe.

After a long silence, Frank said hello.

"Hi, Frank. It's me. I need some information," she said. "If somebody said he had an appointment with the head honcho at the Auto Federation, who would he be talking about?"

"Hmm," said Frank over the line. "Henri is on the board, but I think Pierre Desmoulins is the guy who pretty much runs things."

"Do you have the number over there?" she asked.

He read her a telephone number he had in his notebook. "Give it a try. If you don't get him, let me know," he added. "Joe and I will be at Henri's office this morning. He's insisted that we take some time off to check out his race cars. But we may go by the Federation garage later."

"I'll call if I need you," Nancy told him. "Have fun."

Emily waited until Nancy hung up, then said, "I have to get to work. You'll tell me the instant you find out anything?"

"Definitely," Nancy reassured her.

After Emily left, Nancy dialed the number Frank had given her. A man picked up after five rings. When Nancy asked for Mr. Desmoulins, the man said, "This is he."

"Mr. Desmoulins, my name is Nancy

Drew," she began. "I'm with the film company of *Dangerous Loves.* I understand that our still photographer, Jack Parmenter, came to see you yesterday morning. Is that right?"

There was a long silence before the man said, "Yes, he did. He wanted to show me some of his work, some photos that he hoped to sell to the Federation."

"Can you tell me what happened?" Nancy asked.

"I told him that his work was very good, but that we didn't need him. We use a local photographer."

"Did he say where he was going?"

After a shorter silence, Desmoulins said, "Actually, I was just leaving the Federation's temporary headquarters here myself. He asked for a ride to the Latin Quarter, near City Hall. He did not say where he was going."

Nancy thought quickly. City Hall was just across from the basilica. Jack must have been on his way to work, but for some reason he never arrived.

"Did you notice whether he had his camera bag with him?" Nancy asked.

"He had only an envelope with the photos," Pierre Desmoulins told her. "But why do you ask all these questions? Is there something wrong?"

"Jack didn't show up for work yesterday or

today," Nancy said. "Jack's friends are worried about him."

"Perhaps he went home, to California," said Desmoulins. "Many people do not much like Quebec winters. Will you excuse me? I have a call on the other line."

After she hung up, Nancy sat staring absently at the telephone, thinking. Where was Jack's equipment? Nancy was sure that she hadn't seen his camera bag at the studio or in his hotel room.

Her thoughts were interrupted by somebody rapping on the door. When she opened it, she found a boy standing there, wearing a cap that said Château Frontenac. Handing her an Express Mail envelope, he said, "This just came in for Mr. Grant Shulman." Then he left.

Nancy glanced down at the slip on the envelope. The initials OCP were typed in the space for company name.

A second later the trailer door swung open, and the envelope was grabbed from Nancy's hands.

"That's mine," Grant barked. "I told that stupid desk clerk not to send it over. What are you doing here? This area's off-limits to visitors."

Nancy eyed him coolly. "Emily said I could make a phone call," she explained. "I was just leaving."

"Emily seems to be giving you and your friend the run of the place," Grant said, glaring at Nancy. "This is a movie set, not a theme park."

What a grouch, thought Nancy, following him out. After pulling the office door shut, she went to look for Bess.

She finally spotted her friend near the ice castle, talking to a seven-foot snowman. Nancy remembered seeing his picture on all the posters for Winter Carnival.

"Hi, Nancy," Bess called. "Come meet my new friend. This is Bonhomme Carnaval."

"Enchanté, mademoiselle," the snowman said in a muffled voice. He bowed comically.

"He's the mascot of Winter Carnival," Bess explained with a giggle. "He gets to give out the prize for the best ice sculpture and crown the Carnival Queen and all that."

"And have my picture taken with all our charming visitors," Bonhomme Carnaval added.

"Too bad I don't have my camera with me," Nancy said, laughing.

"Places, please!" someone called. "Snowman? Snowman! We need you over here!"

Bonhomme Carnaval went over and sat in a thronelike chair in front of the snow castle. Extras formed a circle around him and started to dance.

"And—action!" David Politano called.

Marguerite walked slowly past the dancers. A moment later Dennis ran up to her. "You can't just walk away like that," he said in a voice that sizzled with passion.

She turned to him with tears in her eyes. "I must," she said. "Don't you see? Our worlds are too different. The gulf between us is too wide. It is better to say goodbye now, before the sweetness of our love turns bitter in our mouths."

A sniffling sound made Nancy look around. Brent Moore was wiping his glove across his cheek. When he noticed Nancy, he looked down, as if ashamed.

Could he really have been moved to tears by that dopey dialogue? If so, there was only one possible explanation—he had to be in love with Marguerite!

But why keep their romance a secret?

After David took the cast through three takes of the scene without a pause, the folk-dancing extras looked ready to collapse. They broke into cheers when David announced a half-hour break.

Before everyone scattered, the director called out Billy Fitzgerald's name. Nancy was surprised when the scriptwriter appeared from a small group of people gathered near the castle sculpture. It was the first time she'd seen him since Jack's disappearance.

"*Not* another script change," Billy said loudly.

"There are still a few minor adjustments," David replied. "We can do them in ten minutes. Let's go to the office."

Nancy grabbed Bess's arm. "Come on," she said in a low voice. "This is our chance to check out Billy's hotel room."

"Why?" Bess asked blankly.

"Don't you remember the matchbook I found in Jack's room? It could be important."

The two girls flagged down a passing taxi, and within minutes were standing on the sidewalk in front of the Auberge des Remparts.

Inside, a young man with dark, slicked-back hair and a thin mustache was standing behind the desk. "May I help you?" he asked.

Nancy made it obvious that she was looking around. "May we talk privately?" she asked, raising an eyebrow dramatically.

The man shrugged and said, "Yes, of course. This way, please."

He led them through an archway to a small sitting room and gestured for them to sit down.

"This must be in strict confidence," Nancy began. "One of your guests is being considered for an important honor—the novelist and screenwriter, Billy Fitzgerald. I've been asked to check to make sure that nothing will come out that might embarrass him or those who have honored him. You can understand how important that is."

The concierge seemed to study Nancy and Bess with newfound respect. "Yes, of course," he said.

Great! Nancy thought. He was buying the story. "We heard that a photographer for a notorious scandal sheet was stalking Mr. Fitzgerald. Have you seen anyone with a camera hanging around?"

"We have many tourists, of course," the clerk replied. "Most of them bring cameras."

"The man I mean is a professional. We're told that he is tall and thin, with blond, spiky hair." Nancy gave him Jack's description.

"I've seen no one like that," the concierge said after thinking a moment.

"Have you seen or heard anything concerning Mr. Fitzgerald that you think I should know about?" Nancy said. "Anything the least bit suspicious or out of the ordinary?"

"Why, no, not at all," the man replied. He became a little wary. "Mr. Fitzgerald has been a perfect guest."

"Would you mind showing me his room?"

Nancy asked. "Just a peek in the door, so that I can put in my report that I saw it?"

The concierge's manner cooled off abruptly. "I'm sorry," he said. "That's quite out of the question. Our guests trust us, and we do everything we can to deserve that trust."

"Of course," Nancy said, stifling her disappointment. Bess tugged once at Nancy's sleeve. She was silently forming some word with her lips, but Nancy couldn't make out what it was.

"Excuse me, I must get back to my post," the concierge said.

The moment he left them, Bess said, "Nan, I just saw Danielle Rocheville! You know, the one who was Snake Junot's girlfriend. She came out of the hallway, right across the lobby from us, and walked out the front door."

"Are you sure it was her?" Nancy asked.

Bess nodded vigorously. "I saw her face."

"Did she see you?" Nancy demanded.

"I'm sure she didn't," Bess answered. "She didn't even look this way."

"I wonder if there's any connection between her and Billy?" Nancy mused. "Well, Danielle could be staying here, I guess. Bess—keep that guy busy for a couple of minutes, okay?"

Bess grinned. "Sure! I'll just ask him to tell me about the sights of Quebec."

While Bess and the concierge chatted, Nancy strolled over to the hallway from which Bess had seen Danielle emerge. It was short, with only four doors leading off it. They were numbered seven through ten.

Coming back out of the hallway, Nancy saw that Bess had maneuvered the concierge over near the front door. He was gesturing with his arms, as if giving her directions. Nancy quickly checked out the hotel register. Billy was in Room Fourteen, on the second floor. As for Rooms Seven through Ten, one was empty, and the other three were occupied by M. and Mme. Broussard, J. Malone, and Peter Mills. Danielle Rocheville's name wasn't listed on the register at all.

Nancy turned away from the desk and jotted down the names in her book. Now all she had to figure out was which room Danielle had been visiting, and why.

"I'm psyched to check out the Dussault race cars," Joe said as he and Frank entered the Dussault Motors building.

Joe followed Frank up to the second floor and to Henri's office.

"We're a little early," Frank said, checking his watch. "Henri said he'd be at one of the Dussault warehouses until ten-thirty. It's only a quarter after now."

Frank paused as the door to Henri's office opened. François Volnay stepped out with a manila file in his right hand. Surprise showed in Volnay's eyes when he saw the Hardys. Then he nodded stiffly and started down the hall toward the staircase.

"Is Henri here?" Frank asked him.

"Ah, no," Volnay replied hesitantly.

Joe gave the former race car driver a sharp look. Why was François so jumpy?

"I was, um, getting some papers for him," François continued.

As he held up the file folder, it slipped out of his hand and sailed to the floor. Papers scattered all over the hall floor. François started to kneel to pick them up. He gave a grunt of pain. Apparently his injury made it hard for him to kneel.

"Here, I'll get them for you," Joe offered automatically. It was a golden opportunity to see what was in the file.

"No, no, please," François said quickly. But Joe and Frank were already gathering the papers and putting them back in the folder.

When they were finished, François took the folder and hurried down the stairs.

"Okay," said Joe when he guessed François was out of earshot. "Did you see anything?"

Frank gave him a grim smile. "A printout of the file I was looking at yesterday, of the prize fund bank account. Henri said he wasn't going to tell anyone about the embezzlement and that he was the only one who even looked at the bank statements."

Joe's mind was racing. "That means that the only reason François would have to look into the account is if he's stealing the money himself!"

Chapter Thirteen

THERE WAS NO receptionist or secretary to stop him, so Frank pushed open the door to Henri's office.

"Let's see if we can find out what Volnay was up to," he told his brother.

Joe went to the computer terminal. "Still warm," he reported.

Frank opened the closet door. "The printer's warm, too," he said, touching it. "François probably printed out the prize fund records just now."

He and Joe both turned as the door opened and Henri walked in.

"Ah, good, you are here," the older man said with a smile.

Taking a deep breath, Frank plunged in and told Henri about their suspicions of François.

"I refuse to believe it!" Henri said instantly. "I have known François Volnay for ten years. There is no one in the world I trust more than him."

"Did you authorize him to call up that file and make a copy of it?" Frank asked Henri. "Is that part of his job?"

Conflicting emotions chased one another across Henri's face. "No, I did not," he said finally. "I have no idea why he would do such a thing.

"But if he had asked me," Henri continued, "I would have said yes in a moment. I have complete confidence in François."

"Did you get in touch with the bank this morning and change the access code from that account?" Frank asked.

"Certainly," Henri replied. "It was the first thing I did."

"Good. So the rest of the prize money is safe now." Frank hesitated before asking, "Would you mind telling us what your old access code was? I've been trying to figure out how the embezzler got hold of it."

To Frank's surprise, Henri's cheeks turned

pink. "I chose something very simple—my birthdate. Eleven, twenty-eight."

"How many of your friends and business associates are likely to know your birthdate?" Frank asked.

"Why, all of them," Henri replied. "When I became fifty-five, people from the factory and the Auto Federation offered me a wonderful *fête d'anniversaire.* Even the mayor made an appearance, and there were photos in the newspaper the next day."

Frank raised his eyes to the ceiling. Almost anybody in the city of Quebec could have cracked Henri's code!

"I hope the new number you picked is a little harder to figure out," Joe remarked.

"I believe I came up with something rather clever. It's—" Henri began.

Frank held up his hand. "If you don't mind," he said, "we'd rather not know. And I don't think you ought to share it with anybody else, either."

"No, of course not," Henri agreed quickly.

The telephone on Henri's desk rang. Henri answered it, listened for a moment, then passed the receiver to Frank.

"Frank, I was hoping I'd find you there," Nancy said. "Could you and Joe come over to our hotel right away?"

"Sure," Frank said. "What's wrong? Has something happened?"

"Not exactly. Not yet, anyway," she replied. "I want to show you something and get your thoughts on it. But it has to be soon. I'd rather not talk about it over the phone."

"We're practically there already," Frank assured her.

"Great, you guys are here," Nancy said, ushering the Hardys into Bess's and her room at the Château Frontenac twenty minutes later.

"At your service," said Joe, grinning. "What's up? Where are Bess and Emily?"

Nancy smiled. "Bess is out buying a new dress for her date with Dennis tonight, and Emily is still working," she answered as she handed Joe an envelope with her name and Château Frontenac typed on it. "This was left at the desk for me." Inside was a folded piece of unlined paper with a message typed on it:

> I can tell you where Jack Parmenter is hiding. Meet me this evening at five on the Promenade des Gouverneurs. Come alone, and do not tell anyone about this. DANGER.

Joe stared at the note. "Where Jack is hiding? What's that supposed to mean?"

Frank read the note and tapped it with his finger. "If you ask me, it's a trap," he said.

"I was thinking the same thing," Nancy said. "The question is, how do I spring it?"

"The Promenade des Gouverneurs," Frank read. "Do you know where that is?"

"It's a walkway that winds along the cliff."

Frank glanced at his watch. "It's dark before five," he pointed out. "There's no way we're letting you go there alone and in the dark. Joe and I will hide somewhere nearby and keep an eye on you. With luck, we'll manage to trap the trappers."

At two minutes to five Nancy went out the front door of the Château Frontenac and walked toward the promenade. The Hardys had left half an hour earlier, to scout the territory and find a good hiding place.

It was a clear night. The moon wasn't yet up, but stars glittered in the sky. Apparently the cold weather made people want to hole up inside where it was warm, because Nancy passed only a few other people on her way to the promenade. There was little chance anyone else would be on the Promenade des Gouverneurs after dark, which was probably exactly what whoever had sent the note was counting on. Nancy was doubly glad she'd thought to call Frank and Joe for backup.

Nancy hesitated at the Promenade des Gouverneurs. It was narrower than she had assumed it would be, and hung on the side of the cliff. One side was bordered by solid rock, the other by a sheer dropoff. Where could Frank and Joe be hiding?

Taking a deep breath, Nancy started along the walk, which plunged down at first. Moments later it turned into a long, steep flight of stairs that hugged the cliff.

In spite of her layered sweaters and down parka, Nancy started to shiver. *Get a grip, Drew!* she ordered herself. Squaring her shoulders, she started up the stairs.

She was about a third of the way up when a man appeared at the head of the stairs, silhouetted against the glow from a nearby streetlight. As he started down the stairs, Nancy saw with a start that there was only a dark blue blur where the man's face should have been. He was wearing a ski mask.

With a sinking feeling, Nancy took a quick look over her shoulder. Just as she had feared, a second man was waiting at the foot of the stairs. She was trapped!

There was no time to wait for help from the Hardys. She didn't even know where they were.

Nancy whirled around. When in doubt, she thought, let gravity work for you. She began to run back down the steps, taking them two and three at a time. The masked man below was waiting for her at the bottom of the stairs, his arms spread wide to block her way.

When Nancy got about ten steps above the man, she gripped the railing with both hands and hurled herself downward, feet first.

An instant later her boots hit something soft and she heard a loud "oof!" The man she had crashed into doubled over and fell to the ground, clutching his stomach. Nancy vaulted over him, then looked up the stairs. The second attacker was about thirty steps up, racing after her. Just then she became aware of the pounding of feet on the walkway behind her.

"Hold on, Nancy, we're coming!" she heard Joe call.

A moment later the Hardys brushed past her. Joe leapt over the attacker Nancy had knocked down and ran up the stairs after the other masked man. Frank collared the thug at the foot of the stairs.

To Nancy's surprise, the fallen masked man reached up in a flash and flipped Frank over onto his back. Before Frank could recover his footing, the thug pushed himself up and ran back along the path. Nancy heard a car start and speed away seconds later.

"Sorry, Nancy," Frank said, getting to his feet. "I should have seen that coming."

"Don't worry about it," she told him. "If it weren't for you and Joe, I might have been in much more serious trouble."

Frank looked up the stairs. "Looks like Joe's guy got away, too," he said glumly, pointing to his brother, who was descending the stairs toward them.

"No luck," Joe announced. "He gave me the slip."

"Well, we learned one thing, anyway," Nancy said. "Those guys obviously weren't about to give me any information about Jack, and they don't like the fact that I'm trying to find him."

The three detectives walked back to the Château Frontenac, where Nancy found a note from Emily waiting for her at the front desk. She wanted to know if Nancy would come with her to go once more through the things Jack had left at the studio.

"Do you mind if we tag along?" Frank asked.

"Sure. The more the merrier," Nancy told him.

She called Emily's room, and a few minutes later the foursome was walking through the City Hall Gardens toward Mike's studio.

"Nancy, you could have been killed!" Emily exclaimed when Nancy told her about the note she'd received and the masked attackers. "Do you really think Jack could be in hiding, like the note said?" she asked.

"It's possible," Nancy answered slowly. "But I think if Jack had willingly disappeared, he would have contacted you."

"But Nancy must be close to finding him," Frank added, "or those guys wouldn't have tried scaring her off that way."

Emily nodded, biting her lip. "That's true."

Light streamed out through the skylight at Mike's studio, but no one answered when they knocked. "Mike said he'd be here," Emily said, frowning.

"Maybe he's in the darkroom and can't hear us," Joe suggested.

Nancy tried the door. It was unlocked. "Anybody home?" she called, pushing it open and going inside.

The studio was a wreck. Books, photos, and equipment were scattered all over the floor. Nancy gasped as she saw a figure on the far side of the room.

It was Mike Adams, and he was lying on his side, tied hand and foot to a wooden chair!

Chapter Fourteen

"MIKE!" EMILY CRIED, rushing over to him.

Frank, Joe, and Nancy were close behind. Together, they untied Mike and helped him to his feet.

"Are you okay?" Emily asked him.

"I've been better," the photographer said wryly. "I don't think they did any permanent damage, though."

"They?" Frank asked.

"Two guys," Mike explained, rubbing the red rope marks on his wrists. "That's all I know. They were both wearing ski masks.

"They charged in, grabbed me, and tied me to the chair before I could stop them. They kept asking me where Jack's negatives were. I told them, but they must not have found what they wanted. After a few minutes they came back and started slugging me. Then they tore the place up and left."

"When did they leave?" Nancy asked.

After a pause Mike said, "Just before five, I think. Yeah—that's right."

"It has to be the same two we just ran into," Nancy told Frank and Joe.

"And that means that Jack's disappearance and the missing negatives are related to your case, not ours," Frank put in. "Otherwise, the hoods would have come after us instead of you."

Nancy frowned. "I wonder if that means the guy who tried to run us down in that car last night was after me, too?"

Joe nodded soberly. "Probably."

Nancy gave another look around the studio. "I wish we had more to go on." Turning to Jack, she asked, "They went into the dark-room, right?"

He nodded.

"When I was here before, I noticed that Jack kept all his negatives and contact sheets in a metal file case in there. Did they take that?"

Mike rubbed his head gingerly. "I don't think so."

"Let's take a look," Frank said.

He and the others followed Nancy into the darkroom. A large metal file case was lying on its side on the counter, with manila folders scattered over the counter and nearby stretches of floor.

The four friends picked up the photos, negatives, and folders and sorted them by date.

"All the folders are here," Nancy announced when they were done. "All but the one from the day Bess and I arrived. But that one was already missing when I came here yesterday."

"That must be why the two guys were so mad," Mike said. "What they came to get wasn't here."

"Do you know what pictures he took that day?" Joe asked.

"Not everything, but that was the morning that David Politano almost went into the river, and that afternoon Dennis and Marguerite were nearly run over."

"Snake Junot's car was blown up that day, too," Joe added. "And Jack was at Junot's press conference just before the explosion."

Nancy's mind clicked away. "Guys, there is something else to run by you," she said. "Bess saw Danielle Rocheville when we were at Billy's hotel this morning."

She dug in her purse and pulled out the slip of paper with the names she'd copied from the hotel register. "Do the names Mr. and Mrs.

Broussard, J. Malone, or Peter Mills mean anything to you?" she asked. "Those are the people who are staying in the hall where Bess saw Danielle."

Frank frowned, shaking his head. "I wouldn't put something sneaky past Danielle," he said. "But none of those names rings a bell."

"Broussard is a pretty common last name in Quebec," Mike told the others.

With a laugh, Nancy said, "Maybe it was just a coincidence that she was there."

"Hey," said Joe, changing the subject. "What about that note you got? Maybe we should try to track down the handwriting."

"It was typed," Nancy reminded him.

"We'll track down the typewriter, then." Joe turned to Emily and asked, "Do a lot of people in the film crew have typewriters?"

"The only one I know of for sure is Billy Fitzgerald's. He made a big deal about the company paying to have his favorite electric typewriter shipped here. He said it was too bulky for him to carry on the plane."

Nancy brushed back her reddish blond hair. "But how can we get a typing sample from it?" she wondered aloud.

"When we wrapped up filming this afternoon," Emily said, "David asked Billy for some rewrites. Billy said he had tickets for a play, and if David wanted rewrites tonight, he could write them himself. So that means—"

"The coast is clear in Billy's room," Nancy finished. "The concierge at the hotel is really protective of his guests, though," she added. "But I think I know just the person to help us get by him."

"Nancy! What are you doing here?" Bess exclaimed. She and Dennis were in a small restaurant around the corner from the Château Frontenac.

"Bess, am I glad you told me where you were going tonight. Listen, I need to borrow you for a few minutes," Nancy told her. "Dennis won't mind, I'm sure."

Bess asked, "Can't it wait?"

"No," Nancy said urgently. She decided to be frank in front of Dennis, since someone had tried to frame him.

"I was wondering about all those questions you guys asked," Dennis said after Nancy and Bess explained their real reason for being in Quebec. "I've never had a date with a detective before," he added with a grin. "Are you sure I can't help?"

"Not this time," Nancy told him. "But I really will get Bess back as fast as I can."

Outside, the two girls joined Frank, Joe, and

Emily, and Nancy explained to Bess what she wanted.

"If we're going to do it, let's get it done fast," Bess said. "I want to get back to my dessert."

At the Auberge des Remparts, Bess went into the lobby alone, while Nancy watched from a recessed alcove just inside the front door. The others waited outside.

Bess walked up to the front desk, smiled and said, "I was passing by, and I just had to come in and tell you how helpful you were this morning. I went to all those places you told me about, and I enjoyed every one of them."

With a pleased nod, the concierge said, "I am very happy, mademoiselle. We are proud of our city, you know."

"When we were in that sitting room this morning, I noticed a lot of old engravings on the walls," Bess continued. "Were those all views of Quebec?"

"Ah, yes, a fine collection," the concierge said. "It is astonishing how much of the city looks the same today as it did a hundred years ago, when the prints were made. Shall I show you what I mean?"

Good thinking, Bess! Nancy thought. As soon as Bess and the concierge went through the archway, Nancy slipped into the lobby and made a dash for the stairs.

She found Room Fourteen halfway down the hall to her left. Nancy tapped lightly, then pressed her ear to the door to listen. Nothing.

Nancy took a plastic credit card from her wallet. After checking to make sure the hallway was empty, she slid the card into the crack between the door and the jamb, just below the lock. A little jiggling, and she heard a satisfying click.

She pushed the door open and slid into the darkened room. She found the light switch, flipped it on, and the first thing she saw was a big old electric typewriter on a low table near the window.

She inserted a piece of paper, and pecked out "Jack Parmenter. Promenade DANGER," then reached into her purse for the note she had received. She held it up next to the freshly typed words.

The typefaces were not a bit alike.

Nancy turned off the typewriter and the overhead light, and slipped out of the room. She paused halfway down the stairs. Hearing Bess's voice coming from the sitting room, she ran the rest of the way down the stairs and across the lobby.

As she slipped past the arched doorway and outside to rejoin the others, Bess was only a few steps behind her.

Emily, Frank, and Joe were waiting just

outside the door, stomping their feet to keep warm.

"Any luck?" Joe asked.

"It's not the typewriter we're looking for," Nancy replied.

Emily's face fell. "Oh. I was really hoping . . ." Her voice trailed off. "There is a typewriter in the production trailer," she added. "Should we check that?"

"Definitely," Nancy told her. "It's still parked at the Place du Carnaval, right? Next to the snow castle? We can drop Bess off on the way."

"My date." Bess sighed. "My dessert!"

Nancy, Frank, Joe, and Emily made their way to the Place du Carnaval. The snow castle and other sculptures sparkled in the light from the street lamps.

After showing her pass to the guard, Emily found her key and led the others into the production trailer.

Nancy had to type only a few letters to know that it wasn't the right typewriter. For one thing, it had the kind of ribbon that could be used only once because it left a permanent imprint in the carbon.

As she was putting the note back in its envelope, her gaze fell on the address: Nancy Drew, Château Frontenac.

"I'm an idiot," she said. "This must have

been typed on a French typewriter. See? The *a* in *Château* has one of those funny hats on it."

The others looked. "I've seen some American typewriters with accents like that," Joe said.

"This one doesn't have them," said Nancy. She looked more closely at the keyboard, then at the ribbon. She could tell what letters she had typed by looking at the ribbon itself. Whoever had used the typewriter right before her had typed the letters OCP.

Nancy frowned, searching her memory. Wasn't that the name of the company that had sent that express envelope to Grant Shulman?

"Does OCP mean anything to any of you?" she asked.

"Sure," said Emily. "Oh! Canada Productions. They wanted to coproduce *Dangerous Loves,* but David turned them down. He didn't think they had the technical ability to carry a big project like ours. He went with someone else." Chuckling, she added, "They didn't much like that."

Nancy lifted the ribbon cassette out of the typewriter and held it up to the light. The letters before OCP were *nt Shulman.* "Can you think of a good reason for Grant to be writing to Oh! Canada?" she asked Emily. "Or getting express packages from them?"

"Grant?" Emily said, surprised. "No, I can't."

"I can," Nancy said grimly. "When somebody important in a company starts exchanging secret messages with a rival company, it usually means dirty work of some kind. I think Grant cut some kind of deal with OCP to wreck this film."

Chapter Fifteen

"THAT WOULD EXPLAIN IT!" Emily cried, comprehension dawning in her brown eyes. "Grant has made one dumb mistake after another in the last few days. Remember, for instance, the flower girl who was in the wrong place? I figured he was simply losing his grip. It never occurred to me that he might be doing it on purpose."

"The question is, can we prove it? I think I may have a plan, but I'll need help," Nancy said.

"We've been away from our case long enough," Frank said apologetically. "Tomorrow we've got to do a thorough check on François Volnay."

"I'm available," Emily added. "What's the plan?"

Nancy's blue eyes sparkled with excitement. "Okay, here's what we're going to do. . . ."

"It's freezing out here," Joe complained early the next morning, banging his gloved hands against the steering wheel to keep them warm.

He and Frank were sitting in their car, which was parked diagonally across the street from François Volnay's house, on a quiet street in the Lower Town.

"We can't turn on the heat without starting the engine," Frank reminded him. "And that might attract Volnay's attention."

Joe nodded. They definitely didn't want to lose François this time, even though Joe wasn't exactly looking forward to proving that Henri's good friend was a criminal.

They had a cold wait of almost half an hour, but finally François came out of his house and climbed into an old car.

"Don't forget," Frank warned Joe. "He may have had to retire because of his stiff leg, but he was a champion driver for years. If he finds out we're following him, that's the last we'll see of him."

"Give me a break," Joe said, jabbing his elbow into Frank's ribs. "Joe Hardy can tail anyone, anywhere. Volnay will never even know we're here."

"If you say so," Frank murmured.

Joe turned his attention to the road, following François up a steep street.

"There's the Frontenac, behind us," Frank said, turning in the passenger seat to look around. "Unless I'm wrong, the park where the movie company is filming is right up ahead. Do you think that's where he's going?"

Joe shrugged. "We'll know soon enough."

But François kept going, passing through another of the city gates and turning onto a wide boulevard. Soon he parked the car and started walking. Joe and Frank let Volnay get a good lead, then followed on foot.

The older man turned up a walk that led to a set of modern buildings built around a courtyard. Joe looked at the sign next to the walk. "'École d'Affaires,'" he read. "That means Business School, doesn't it? What's he doing here?"

"Good question," Frank replied. "Let's go find out."

They followed François inside one of the buildings, where he went to the second floor and entered a half-full classroom. Soon a middle-aged woman with an attaché case entered the room and started to lecture in French.

Joe gave his brother a curious look. "That's weird. François never said anything about going to business school, but it looks like that's exactly what he's doing."

"Henri and Pierre didn't say anything about it, either," said Frank. "I wonder why François would keep something like this from them? Let's stick around for a while."

At last François walked out, and his eyes widened when he saw the Hardys. He made a quick decision to confront them.

"You must have learned that I was not authorized to go into Monsieur Dussault's office, didn't you?" François said before Joe could open his mouth.

"You went into his files, too, didn't you?" Frank accused. "And made copies of the Auto Federation records?"

"It's true," François said. "It's all true."

Joe stared curiously at François. Why was he admitting everything so readily? Didn't he realize he could be implicating himself in Junot's murder?

"Why?" he asked François. "What did you hope to accomplish?"

François glanced around, then lowered his

voice. "I thought with those records and my new skills, I might succeed in uncovering the person who has been stealing from the prize fund."

Frank and Joe were not convinced. Apparently, François sensed their skepticism, too.

"I was in the next office when you told Monsieur Dussault about the stealing," François explained. "I heard everything. It was then that I decided to solve the mystery myself."

"What exactly are you doing here, François?" Frank asked.

François's face reddened, and he turned away. "I am not an educated man," he said. "I became a professional race car driver before I was eighteen. After that, I had no time to learn anything else. But since my accident, I have had all the time in the world."

He hesitated before adding, "Monsieur Dussault is a true friend. He has been kind enough to give me a job with his company. But I want a post that I earn on my own. All this year, I have been taking courses here. In the spring I will have earned my certificate in business. After that, I mean to ask for a position with the Auto Federation, not because of what I once was, but because of what I have made of myself."

Joe glanced at Frank. The man's story seemed genuine, but that didn't mean he didn't kill Junot. In fact, the skills he was learning in business school classes made him an even more likely suspect in the embezzlement.

"How do we know that you weren't stealing the money yourself?" Joe blurted out.

François responded only by reaching into his briefcase and pulling out the prize fund spread sheet. "I have learned a little about electronic funds transfers from my classes," he said. "I printed out the records of the prize fund because I thought that I might find a clue from studying them."

"And did you?" Frank pursued.

"Not yet," François confessed. "Each bank has its own way of coding information about transfers. Without a knowledge of the code, all you have is a string of meaningless numbers. Here," François continued, pointing with his forefinger. "These are the four illicit transfers. These many digits next to them tell much about the transaction, but I cannot decode them."

Frank and Joe studied the numbers François was pointing to.

"The first six numbers seem to be a date," Frank said eventually. "And so do the second six. The dates are one or two days apart in each case."

"You are right!" exclaimed François. "No doubt, the first is the date of the request and the second is the posting date, the date on which the bank actually carried out the request."

"Look," said Joe. "The twelve numbers after that are the same each time."

"Are you sure?" François asked. He counted off the numbers twice. "Then there is my proof!" he exclaimed. "This must be the number of the bank account the money was transferred to."

Joe grabbed his brother's arm. "Let's go find a telephone," he said urgently. "Maybe Henri can ask the people at the bank to trace the account."

François showed them where there was a telephone on the ground floor.

Frank's face was grim when he hung up a few minutes later. "Henri's going to call the bank," he told Joe and François. "He did point out something else when I read him the numbers. The last four digits are the log-on numbers of the computer the request was made from.

"He has a list of all the log-on numbers for the terminals that are hooked into his computer network."

"And the number from the embezzler's computer was on the list?" Joe guessed.

Frank nodded. "That log-on number is assigned to the computer at the Auto Federation garage," said Frank. "The one in Pierre Desmoulins's office."

"Pierre?" François repeated blankly. "But this is terrible! Someone is abusing his confidence by using his terminal to steal from the prize fund!"

"I hate to say this, François," Joe said. "There's a good chance the thief is Pierre himself."

"Do you think this plan will work?" Bess asked in a low voice, studying the people having breakfast in the small café where she and Nancy were sitting.

Nancy reached up and lifted one of her earphones. "It's working so far," she said. "I can hear loud and clear every time Dennis takes a sip of his coffee."

She resettled the earphone in place and adjusted the volume control of the pocket receiver and tape recorder Emily had let her borrow from the film company. They were set to pick up sound from the tiny microphone and battery-powered transmitter hidden in Dennis's jacket.

"It was great of Dennis to agree to help us," Bess said, nodding to the actor a few tables away.

"Stop grinning at him, Bess," Nancy warned, chuckling. "We're supposed to be pretending we don't even know him." She opened her notepad and uncapped a pen. To anyone else, it would look as if she was studying while listening to music on a portable cassette player. "Oops, quiet—I think this is our guy."

From the corner of her eye Nancy could see a man in business clothes standing beside Dennis's table. She pressed the red Record button and started writing.

Nancy gave Bess the thumbs-up sign. She could hear the man's voice perfectly in her earphone.

"Conners?" a gruff voice said.

"That's right," Dennis told the man. "Sit down. You're late. I was starting to wonder."

"I caught the first plane from Montreal after your phone call," the man said.

"Okay, let's make this fast," said Dennis. "I found out about the deal between Grant Shulman and OCP—"

"No names," the man cut in quickly.

"Okay. Between my associate, then, and your firm," Dennis went on. "Never mind how I found out. The point is, I did. And I want in on it. You know who I am. You know how important I am to the project."

After a short pause the man said, "It's a real shame we didn't meet six weeks ago."

"Then it's a deal?" Dennis asked. "I make sure the production is a fiasco, and your company pays me?"

"Nope, no deal," the man replied. "If I'd known you were available a while ago, sure. But we don't need any more help. Our man on the scene has come up with a plan that'll do the trick. By tomorrow, there won't *be* any production."

"No deal?" Dennis said, in a voice full of menace. He really *was* a great actor! "That's not very smart. What's to stop me from telling the authorities what I know? And don't say I'll be sorry if I do. You'll be a lot more sorry, I guarantee it!"

"Hey, take it easy," the man said. He sounded nervous. "All I meant was, we don't need any more help. But we know how to take care of friends. Here, I brought this along for you."

Nancy heard the rustle of paper, then the sound of an envelope being torn open.

"That's pretty generous," the man continued, "considering that all you have to do for it is keep your mouth shut."

"I can live with that," Dennis said. "But this

stunt today, what makes you so sure that it'll do the trick? My associate hasn't shown much talent for this work so far."

"This time *we* set it up," the man replied. "No more horsing around with little mosquito-bite stunts. This one'll make all the papers, even in New York and L.A." He let out a scornful laugh. "And the beauty of it is, no one will catch on. They'll think it's the snake all over again."

"The snake? What does that mean?" Nancy heard Dennis ask. The same question was echoing in her own mind.

"Never mind. You'll see." The man's voice was fading. Nancy risked a glance in the direction of Dennis's table and saw that the man was on his feet now. "Just remember," he said. "Keep this to yourself and you'll be okay. Open your trap, and you're in trouble—very big trouble."

He walked out of the café.

Nancy stopped the tape recorder and took off the earphones.

"What is it, Nan?" Bess demanded. "What did you hear? You're as pale as a ghost!"

"'The snake all over again,'" Nancy repeated, half to herself. "It *can't* mean anything else. But would they dare?"

She looked up as Dennis got up, left some

money on his table, then came over to join them.

"Nancy, did you get what you needed?" he asked.

"The recording's fine. But I'm not nearly as worried about getting good evidence as I am about what that guy said to you."

"What? What did he say?" Bess asked again.

Without answering her friend, Nancy asked Dennis, "What scene of the movie is being shot today?"

"We're back at the race course on the Saint Charles," Dennis replied. "This afternoon, I win the big race."

Nancy frowned. "What about this morning?"

"Oh, I'm not called this morning," Dennis told her. "That's why I was able to help you out. They're filming race scenes. Brent Moore, the stunt driver, is standing in for me."

"Brent is driving this morning?" she exclaimed in horror. "So that's what the guy from OCP meant. All that business about a snake—"

"Nancy, will you please start speaking English," Bess cut in. "What are you talking about!"

"The guy from OCP said something to Dennis about pulling an accident on the set today that would be the snake all over again," Nancy explained in a rush. "He must have been talking about Snake Junot's car exploding."

Bess's face went white. "You don't mean—"

Nancy nodded. "They're planning to put a bomb in Brent's race car!"

Chapter Sixteen

"We have to call the police and the set," Nancy said. "There's not a moment to lose!"

"The phone's over there," said Dennis, pointing to a pay phone in the small hallway leading to the rest rooms.

The three of them jumped up from their table and hurried over to it. Nancy's pulse was racing as she asked the operator to connect her to the police. What if they were too late?

"Hello, police?" she asked when someone answered. "There's a bomb in one of the race cars on the film set of *Dangerous Loves*. It could go off at any time. . . . What? Yes, I'm perfectly serious. My name is Nancy Drew,

I'm a detective from the United States. . . . D-R-E-W . . . No, I did not put the bomb there myself. . . . Look, it doesn't matter how I know. If you people don't get down to the Saint Charles right away, Brent Moore is going to be blown up, just like Snake Junot!"

After Nancy hung up, she said, "I guess they get a lot of crank calls. I hope I convinced them. Dennis, could you give me the number of the telephone in the production trailer?"

Nancy called the number, but it was busy. "Come on," she said, "let's find a taxi and get over to the race course."

They flagged down the first taxi they saw. As the cab started down the slope toward the Saint Charles River, Nancy could hear police sirens in the distance. The sound grew louder. Below them she saw flashing lights speeding toward the ice-racing course.

Nancy sat back and tried to settle her breathing. Panicking wouldn't get them there any faster.

After what seemed like forever, the driver finally braked to a stop behind the police cars next to the river.

They scrambled out of the backseat and ran down the riverbank toward the film crew. Behind them, other members of the company were emerging from the parked trailers to find out what was going on.

The cameras were already set up, Nancy saw. Three cars were in position on the ice. Brent was leaning on the red one that was Dennis's in the movie. The drivers of the other cars were already in their seats. Closer to shore, David Politano was facing half a dozen police officers.

"We're making a movie," he was saying as Nancy, Bess, and Dennis approached. "We can't stop everything because of some crank call—"

"David, *no!*" Dennis shouted, pushing through the crowd and grabbing the director by the shoulders. "You don't understand! Somebody put a bomb in one of those cars!"

David studied Dennis's face for one split second. Then he grabbed the bullhorn and shouted, *"Cut!* Everybody over here, away from those cars! Come on, move it!"

As the drivers and tech crews flew off the ice, two police officers in helmets, face masks, and bulky flak suits walked out over the ice to the nearest of the three cars. They opened the hood and peered in, then one of the officers lay down on the ice and shined a powerful flashlight at the underside of the engine. Apparently, they didn't find anything, because they moved to the second car and then to Brent's.

This time, when the first officer shined the flashlight under the car, his partner made an arm signal to someone on the shore. Two more officers in flak suits staggered out carrying a heavy metal box on a long pole.

Murmurs rippled through the crowd as the police pushed people back.

The seconds ticked by slowly. Finally, the officer who was under the car slid halfway out and handed a small object to his partner. The man carried it slowly over to the steel box, gently placed it inside, and carefully closed the lid. Then he backed away gingerly.

"There *is* a bomb," Bess said with a gasp.

Nancy held her breath as a big truck backed carefully down onto the ice, toward the race car. It was similar to an oil truck, but the tank on the back was covered with layers of thick steel matting. Two officers in flak suits carried the steel box, still on its long pole, over to the back of the truck and maneuvered it through a small opening. The door was gently fastened and the truck pulled away, siren blasting.

Everyone on the set began talking at once. David looked at Dennis and Nancy. "Thanks for saving me from making a big mistake," he told them.

"Excuse me, can you tell me if Mademoiselle Drew is here?" a gray-haired man in a leather trench coat asked.

Nancy stepped forward. "I'm Nancy Drew."

"I'm Inspector Bertholet," the man said. "I

understand that you reported this incident. May I ask if you know who is responsible."

Nancy's gaze fell immediately on Grant Shulman. He was standing just a few feet away, staring at her as if she were poison.

"Mademoiselle Drew?" the inspector prompted.

It was time to lay her cards on the table. "I'm a private investigator," she began. "I was invited here because someone has been trying to wreck the filming of *Dangerous Loves.* I just found out that the person responsible for the sabotage is the assistant director, Grant Shulman. He's been working with a rival company called Oh! Canada Productions."

"Grant, you worthless piece of garbage!" David shouted, storming over to the terrified assistant director.

A police officer restrained David while two others took up positions on either side of Grant.

"This morning," Nancy continued, "I learned that OPC, with Grant Shulman's help, had planted a bomb in one of the stunt cars. They probably hoped the police would think this explosion was linked with the bombing of André Junot's race car three days ago."

"It's only a smoke bomb," Grant protested. "It's totally harmless."

Nancy studied his face. Grant seemed genuinely convinced that the bomb wasn't dangerous. Still, they'd have to wait for the official report before they would know for sure.

"Then you admit you put it there, you backstabber!" David shouted. "How could you? If it weren't for me, you would have been out of the industry years ago! And this is the way you repay me?"

"I, repay *you?"* Grant retorted. "You've done everything you could to keep me down. Where would you be now if you hadn't stolen *Shady Hollow* from me?"

"The producers chose me to direct that film," David said in a gentler tone. "It had nothing to do with keeping you down."

"Grant?" Nancy said, stepping forward. "You *were* responsible for all those accidents, weren't you? You removed the Danger sign and released the brake on the stunt car."

"And what about the firecracker that was thrown at our carriage the other night?" Bess added.

"That was all me," Grant admitted.

Emily pushed through the crowd. "Where's Jack?" she cried, tears streaming down her cheeks. "What have you done with him?"

Grant was obviously bewildered. "Jack? You mean, our still photographer? I didn't do anything with him. I thought he'd quit."

"Did you send two thugs after me last

night?" Nancy asked. "Or try to run me and my friends down with a sports car the night before?"

"Thugs? Sports cars? Of course not," Grant replied. "Why would I? I didn't know you were a detective."

Nancy was almost positive that he was telling the truth. But then, who *had* been behind those attacks? And why?

At that moment one of the officers spoke to Inspector Bertholet. He turned to Grant and said, "Monsieur Shulman? The initial report says your bomb contained enough plastique to blow the car into very small pieces and kill anyone within ten meters of it."

Nancy felt a sick feeling in her stomach. Ten meters—that was almost thirty feet! Brent, the other stunt drivers, the camera and sound crews—they all would have been killed.

"They told me it was a s-smoke bomb," Grant sputtered. "You've got to believe me. I wouldn't—" His voice rose to a scream.

"Take him away," Inspector Bertholet said. "And make sure that he is seen by a doctor."

"I can't believe no one knows where Jack is!" Emily wailed, collapsing next to Nancy on the small couch in the production trailer. She, Nancy, Bess, and Dennis had just finished giving statements to the police. Filming had been postponed until the next day—the day of New Year's Eve.

"It's been three days," Emily continued. "He could be—"

"Isn't there anything we can do?" Bess asked, sitting down in a metal chair next to Dennis.

Nancy's heart went out to Emily. "We won't give up," she said firmly.

"I still believe his disappearance might have something to do with Snake Junot's death," Nancy said. "We know he took photos of Junot's car just minutes before it blew up." She let out a sigh of frustration. "If only we knew where they are."

"Jack developed those rolls of film the night before he vanished, right?" said Bess.

Nancy nodded. "We can guess that he took them with him the next morning. Otherwise, they would still be in the darkroom. But according to Pierre, the only thing Jack brought to his appointment at the Auto Federation was an envelope of enlargements. He must have left the negatives and contact sheets somewhere else."

Emily was now staring open-mouthed at something behind Nancy. "The supply cabinet!" Emily said excitedly. "Why didn't I think of it before?"

"What supply cabinet?" Nancy asked.

"That one." Emily pointed to a metal cabinet with double doors at the far end of the trailer. "We keep paper and gaffer's tape and supplies in it. Jack always locked his gear in there during lunch breaks or whenever he didn't want to haul it around with him. Sometimes he left his camera bag there overnight."

Nancy sprang to her feet. "Do you have the key to it?"

Emily held up a huge ring from which dozens of keys dangled. Nancy, Bess, and Dennis crowded around as Emily found the key and opened the locker door.

"There!" Emily crowed triumphantly, pointing to the bottom shelf, where one corner of a black nylon camera bag was visible. "That's it!"

She pulled the bag out and held it up.

A nine-by-twelve-inch manila envelope was stuck in the back pocket of the bag, Nancy saw. Taking the envelope, she opened it and pulled out a stack of negatives and contact sheets.

"Jack must have left this here before he went to meet Pierre Desmoulins," Nancy guessed. "Is there a magnifying glass around?"

Emily unzipped the camera bag and found one inside.

"Jack's disappearance must be related to the bombing of Junot's car," Nancy said. "So let's concentrate on those rolls of film."

"Here's Junot talking to somebody with a mike," she said excitedly when she got to the third contact sheet. "Junot with his arm around Marguerite—Junot waving to the crowd. Hold it—"

She passed the contact sheet and magnifying glass to Bess and said, "There, in the shadows, what do you see?"

"Behind Junot is a garage with the door open. There's a race car inside. . . . Someone's on the ground next to it, reaching underneath. He has something in his hand."

"The bomb!" Dennis exclaimed. "That's the person who murdered Junot."

Emily gasped. "He took Jack, too. I know it! Who is it, Bess?"

"He's wearing a leather jacket and a beret—I know! It's the guy from the Auto Federation who was driving the car Frank and Joe were in the day Junot was killed!" Bess cried.

"Pierre Desmoulins," Nancy said, snapping her fingers. "We'd better tell Frank and Joe about this. I think we just solved their murder case."

Chapter Seventeen

FRANK LET OUT a whistle as he and Joe leaned over the contact sheet.

"That's Pierre, all right," he said to Nancy.

"So he's a thief *and* a murderer," Joe added, shaking his head in disgust. Seeing the blank look on everyone's face, he explained how he and Joe had traced the illegal fund transfers to Pierre's computer. "When you called, we were just waiting to get confirmation from Henri's bank that the embezzled money was transferred to his account," he finished.

"I think we just figured out the pattern of those two-thousand-dollar withdrawals, too," said Frank. "Junot must have found out about Pierre's embezzling and started to blackmail him. Pierre chose not to pay, and killed him instead."

"What a creep!" Bess said angrily.

"But what about Jack?" Emily put in, biting her lip. "How could this Desmoulins guy know that he happened to take a picture of him planting the bomb? I mean, someone else could have seen him, too, right? Why did the guy have to kidnap Jack?"

"Jack must have showed the picture to him," Nancy guessed. "The morning he disappeared, he went over to the Auto Federation to show Pierre Desmoulins his work." She tapped the incriminating frame on the contact sheet. "This must have been one of the shots he made enlargements of. He probably didn't see Pierre in it."

"But Pierre saw it," Joe added. "He knew he was in terrible danger, and must have abducted Jack on the spot, destroyed the print, and started doing everything he could to locate the negative."

"Then the two thugs who searched the studio were working for Pierre?" Bess asked.

"They must have been," Nancy told her. "And I bet they're the same guys who attacked me on the stairs."

"I guess the real question now is how to nab

Pierre and ensure that we get Jack back safe and sound," Frank said.

Nancy nodded. "First of all, I think we'd better call in the police. That Inspector Bertholet seemed competent."

"He's a friend of Henri's," Joe put in.

"Good," said Nancy, "because we need someone we're sure will move quietly and carefully, to keep from alarming Desmoulins."

Nancy was about to call the police station, when the telephone rang.

"Nancy, this is Marguerite Laforet," the voice on the other end said. "I cannot thank you enough for what you did today. If not for you, my dear Brent would be dead, and I would be the most miserable person on the earth."

"That's okay," Nancy said.

"I am calling from the airport," Marguerite went on. "Brent and I are leaving in a few moments for Toronto, where we will be married. I realized today that we must not put it off any longer. Who knows what tomorrow will bring?"

"Congratulations to both of you," Nancy said sincerely. "But why go to Toronto? Why not get married here?"

After a short silence, Marguerite said, "You will think me a terrible coward, I know. Brent is Anglo, and I am French Canadian. I don't care about that one bit, but my family is very old-fashioned. It will take time to prepare them for this marriage. And if we were married in Quebec, or even Montreal, someone would notice and spread the news. Already I am afraid that Danielle Rocheville suspects and will say something."

"Danielle? Why?" Nancy asked.

"She was behind us in the line at the airline ticket office today," Marguerite replied.

"Oh. What about *Dangerous Loves?"* Nancy asked the actress. "You're not planning to quit, are you?"

Marguerite laughed. "Of course not. I'll be back tomorrow morning."

Nancy hung up the phone, then called the police. After being placed on hold, she was finally put through to Inspector Bertholet.

"We must discuss this situation in more detail," the inspector told her once she had told him about the incriminating photograph and her suspicions that Jack was being held by Pierre Desmoulins. "Will you and your friends come to my office?"

"We'd better not," Nancy told him. "Desmoulins or one of his men might see us arriving at police headquarters and do something rash."

She glanced at her watch. "Would you be

willing to meet at my room at the Frontenac, at noon?"

"Very well," the inspector said.

Nancy turned back to the others. "I think Frank, Joe, and I had better handle this on our own," she said.

Emily, Bess, and Dennis began to protest, but Nancy held up a hand. "Remember, if we're right, this guy is a killer as well as a kidnapper. It's too dangerous."

"Well," Dennis said after a long silence, "there's a place near here called Montmorency Falls. It's supposed to be really spectacular at this time of year. Maybe we could go there."

"Well, if we can't help, we might as well do something that will take our minds off our trouble," Bess said. "What do you say, Emily, will you come?"

Nancy was relieved when Emily nodded.

The inspector listened to Nancy and the Hardys' story and scrutinized the contact sheet. "This is excellent. With this evidence, I can arrest Desmoulins this very day."

"But what about Jack?" Nancy asked.

"Because of him, I will wait. I will give you until tomorrow evening—New Year's Eve—to find your friend. My officers will search also. If we do not have results by then, I will have to move. I expect you to keep me informed of what you are doing. Is that agreed?"

The three young detectives nodded.

"Very well," Inspector Bertholet said, getting to his feet. "Good hunting."

There was a short silence after the door closed. Finally, Joe said, "What do we do now? Any ideas of how we can find out where Desmoulins is hiding Jack?"

"What if we offered to turn over that negative in return for Jack's safe return?" Nancy suggested.

Frank shook his head. "Pierre wouldn't fall for it. Everybody knows you can make copies of a negative."

"What about this?" Nancy said slowly. "Desmoulins doesn't yet know that we're working together, right?" Frank and Joe nodded. "Suppose I meet him alone? You guys could be hiding nearby and follow him when he leaves. He might lead you straight to Jack."

"Too dangerous," said Frank.

"Not if I meet him somewhere very public," Nancy told him. "How about the lobby of the Frontenac? He wouldn't dare try anything with so many people around. And it would be easy for you and Joe to make yourselves inconspicuous, too."

Joe said, "I like it. I can be waiting in the car,

and, Frank, you can be on foot. That way we've got him covered. Let's give it a shot."

Frank still didn't look convinced. "But how are you going to get him to agree to a meeting?" he wanted to know.

"I'll just let him think that I'm planning to blackmail him," Nancy replied. "I'll tell him I have Jack's negative and offer to sell it to him. He'll believe me. Crooks love to think that everyone else is crooked, too."

Two hours later Nancy was sitting in one of the leather armchairs that dotted the lobby of the Château Frontenac and wondering if Pierre would show up at all. On the telephone he had sounded very wary, but she hadn't left him much choice. She said she was prepared to send the negative to the police if he didn't meet her terms.

Nancy tensed as she recognized Pierre Desmoulins.

She stood up and walked toward him. She had given him a vague description of herself over the phone, but there was no reason that he should recognize her.

"Mr. Desmoulins?" she said. "I am Nancy Drew."

He gave her a cold look. "You are very young to be going into this sort of work," he said.

"I'm old enough to know what that picture means," Nancy replied. "And smart enough to know how to take advantage of it."

"Greedy, perhaps, but not so smart," Desmoulins said. "Are you alone in this?"

"Of course," she told him. "Why should I have to share my take?"

He gave her a smile that did not reach his eyes. "And your friend, the photographer?" he asked. "What if I offer him to you, instead of money?"

Nancy shrugged. "He's not my friend," she replied. "I hardly know him."

"I see. What a shame we did not meet under other circumstances, Nancy Drew. I think we might have found each other congenial."

Nancy worked very hard to hide her shudder.

"Very well," Desmoulins continued. "What do you propose?"

"I'll give you the negative for five thousand dollars," Nancy said. "U.S. dollars, not Canadian."

He gave her an icy look. "I do not keep such large sums on hand," he said. "I will call you here when I am ready to proceed."

Without another word, he turned and walked out of the hotel.

* * *

Frank watched the meeting between Nancy and Pierre from the shelter of a rack of paperback books in the hotel newsstand. Pierre's sudden departure, after such a short time, took him by surprise. He hurried after the man, but stopped in the hotel's entrance because Pierre was only a hundred feet away. He was leaning on the railing and looking out at the river.

Frank risked a quick glance at their rental car, which appeared to be empty. But he knew that Joe was in it and ready to move in an instant.

What was Pierre waiting for? Was he meeting his accomplices, to plan some action against Nancy?

Pierre straightened up from the railing, walked briskly to the little building at the edge of the cliff and went inside.

"Of course," Frank muttered to himself, pushing through the hotel doors and breaking into a run. "The funicular!"

As he neared the edge, he saw that one of the glass-walled elevator cars was just starting down the side of the cliff. The other, far below, was beginning its slow journey to the top. Pierre was nowhere in sight. No doubt he had made it into the descending car. His timing had been perfect.

Frank waved an arm above his head. Immediately Joe pulled away from the curb and sped over. "He's on the funicular," Frank shouted, hurling himself into the front seat. "Quick, down the hill!"

Joe made a screeching turn onto a narrow street that passed through one of the city gates then wound steeply downhill.

"Stop!" Frank yelled. He was jolted forward as Joe obeyed, pulling over next to a steep staircase that led down the cliff. "Those are the stairs we took to that restaurant the other night. They lead right down to the funicular station. I'll run down on foot, you drive, and we'll corner him at the bottom."

Jumping out, Frank set off at a run. He soon understood why they were called Breakneck Stairs. The stone treads varied just enough in height and width to force him to concentrate on every step.

Finally he rounded a bend in the stairway and below him saw the historic house that was now the lower station of the funicular. Pierre was just stepping out of the doorway. Frank ducked back as Pierre glanced up the stairs, but it was too late. He had spotted him.

Joe, hurry! Frank urged silently.

Frank was still twenty feet away when a powerful motorcycle sped up to the curb, the rider's face hidden by a dark visor. Pierre swung himself onto the back of the motorcycle, and it roared out of sight a second later.

"Let's face it," Nancy told Frank and Joe a half hour later. "He was two steps ahead of us the whole way."

She slumped back on her bed, while the Hardys settled on Bess's bed.

"Pierre sensed that it might be a trap and had his escape route all planned out," Joe added. "I just wish—"

The telephone on the bedside table rang, and Nancy reached over and grabbed it.

"No more little games, Nancy Drew," Pierre Desmoulins said over the line. "Listen very carefully. I will say this only once. Tomorrow, New Year's Eve, you will go to the costume ball that the film company and Auto Federation are sponsoring. You and your friends must convince Henri Dussault to give you all that is left of the prize fund money. Put it in a box and wrap it in purple paper with a pink ribbon. Bring it to the ball and place it under the Christmas tree at midnight."

"But wait! What if—" Nancy began.

"Do exactly as I say," Desmoulins cut in sharply. "If you do not, you will never see Jack Parmenter alive again!"

Chapter Eighteen

"How do I look?" Bess asked the following evening at ten o'clock. Standing at the foot of her bed, she twirled for Nancy.

"Terrific," Nancy replied, grinning at her friend. "You make a perfect Jeanette MacDonald. Straight out of one of those musical movies from the thirties."

Bess was wearing an off-the-shoulder ballgown in white and pink, with a very full skirt and what looked like a whole florist's shop worth of pink satin rosebuds scattered across it. She'd curled her blond hair into ringlets and placed a white straw hat on her head.

There was a knock on the door. When Bess answered it, Dennis was standing there in the full dress uniform of the Royal Canadian Mounted Police.

"Nelson Eddy, at your service, ladies," Dennis said. "Miss MacDonald, you look ravishing this evening." He looked over at Nancy and added, "And so do you, Miss, er . . ."

Nancy felt her cheeks grow warm. Why on earth had she let Frank talk her into wearing this ridiculous Turkish harem dress, not to mention enough eye makeup to outfit a drugstore!

"I'm supposed to be Mata Hari," she said. "She was a famous spy, a very long time ago."

"Very appropriate," said Dennis, smiling. "Shall we go? My canoe is double-parked."

Before leaving the room, Nancy picked up a shopping bag that contained a box wrapped in purple paper and tied with a pink ribbon.

"A present?" Dennis joked. "You're a little late, Nancy. Tonight is New Year's Eve, not Christmas."

She gave him a smile but said nothing. After the telephone call from Desmoulins the evening before, she, Joe, and Frank agreed to restrict the knowledge of the payoff to as few people as possible.

The group walked to Emily's room and knocked on the door.

"Darling!" Dennis exclaimed when she opened the door. "You're too, *too* Hollywood for words!"

Emily was wearing a platinum blond wig, a slinky floor-length dress covered with red sequins, a white fake-fur coat, and sunglasses studded with rhinestones.

"Thanks, Dennis," Emily said wearily. "Bess, Nancy, you look great."

When she took off the sunglasses for a moment, Nancy saw that her eyes were red from crying.

As the four of them made their way to the elevator, Nancy put an arm around Emily's shoulders. "Don't worry, Emily," she whispered. "I'm sure we'll catch Pierre and find Jack tonight." She hoped she sounded more confident than she felt.

Emily nodded, but she didn't look very hopeful.

The costume party was taking place in the Château Frontenac's grand ballroom. The first thing Nancy saw when they got there was a banner over the entrance with the words *Réveillon au Moulin Rouge* on it. On either side of the doorway were paintings of cancan dancers with an old-fashioned red windmill behind them.

"I've heard of the Moulin Rouge," Bess said. "I even rented the tape of the movie one time. But what does the other part mean?"

"*Réveillon* is the French word for a late-night party," Dennis explained. "Especially one on New Year's Eve. I guess we're supposed to be in Paris at the turn of the century."

The set designers from *Dangerous Loves* had done a great job of decorating the ballroom. All around the walls were large canvas flats with Parisian scenes painted on them.

Then Nancy saw something that made her heart sink. There wasn't just one Christmas tree—there were *four* of them! Which one should she leave her "present" under?

"Oh, look, that's Danielle, dressed as a cowgirl," said Bess, breaking into Nancy's thoughts. "Someone better warn Joe," she joked.

Nancy spotted the petite, auburn-haired woman at the refreshment table. "That's quite a convincing six-shooter she's packing. It almost looks real. There's David, too."

He was wearing jodhpur pants and a sport coat, with a beret at a jaunty angle on his head and a short riding crop in his hand. Except for the ponytail, he was the perfect image of an old-time Hollywood director.

Emily giggled and said, "I guess I'd better go tell him how great he looks."

"Shall we dance?" Dennis asked Bess.

They stepped out onto the dance floor as Nancy began to scan the crowd. She didn't think Desmoulins would trust anyone to pick up a box containing over two hundred thousand dollars in cash. No, he would come himself—but dressed as whom? A character that allowed him to hide his face, probably, but there were lots of those. From where she was standing, Nancy could see a masked Zorro, a Lone Ranger, a hooded executioner, two Ninja Turtles, and three Phantoms of the Opera.

"Aha, Watson," a familiar voice said from behind her about an hour later. "Unless I miss my guess, here is our client now."

Nancy turned around. She grinned when she saw the Hardys. Frank was wearing a tweed deerstalker hat and a long overcoat. Clamped between his teeth was an enormous calabash pipe, and in his left hand he carried a magnifying glass. Joe was much less convincing, in a white hospital jacket with the name *Watson* crudely printed over the pocket. Even the stethoscope around his neck didn't help much.

"Sherlock Holmes and Dr. Watson, I presume?" Nancy guessed.

"Quite right," Joe replied with a phony British accent.

Leaning close to Nancy, Frank added in an undertone, "Twenty minutes until midnight. Do you have the box?"

She lifted her shopping bag and showed it to him. "Right here," she said. Pointing out the four Christmas trees, she asked, "Which one do you think I'm supposed to put the package under?"

"The one near the refreshment table is the biggest," Joe pointed out.

"Thanks, Joe," said Nancy. "I'll leave the box under that one."

Frank took the calabash pipe from his mouth and said, "Let's get a bite to eat."

The three made their way through the crowd to the table. Henri Dussault was there, spreading pâté on a bit of French bread.

"I am very upset by this business," he said. "To find out that someone I have known for years is capable of such evil—that is hard. Do you see that cake?" he added, pointing.

It would be hard to miss, Nancy thought. It was in the shape of a race car, with bright yellow frosting.

"We ordered that especially with André Junot in mind," Henri explained. "At last year's banquet, after he won the championship, he complained that all desserts contained chocolate, which always made him sick. So now we have a special cake with no chocolate, and Junot is not here to enjoy it."

"It's funny what he said about that cake," Joe commented. "When Bess interviewed Danielle, I could've sworn that she said she had baked a chocolate cake for Junot's birthday."

Nancy stared at him. "Joe, are you sure?"

"Yeah," he replied, nodding. "She said it was his favorite."

Suddenly a few more pieces of the puzzle came together. "Listen, Joe," Nancy said urgently, "if you'd been involved with some guy for almost a year, don't you think you'd know that he was allergic to chocolate?"

"Yeah, but why would she lie about being involved with Junot?" Joe asked.

"Because she's really hooked up with Pierre!" Frank answered. "It makes complete sense. Danielle made that scene with Junot right when he was about to check over his car, remember? The whole thing was a diversion."

"Not only that," Nancy added excitedly, "but Marguerite said she saw Danielle at the airline ticket office yesterday. I bet she was buying tickets for their getaway."

"I don't see her now, though," Joe said. "I wonder if she's making the pickup for Pierre?"

Nancy barely heard what he said. Something else was tugging at her mind. They were still overlooking something.

Frank and Joe were still talking, but Nancy tuned them out. She let her mind wander.

The Moulin Rouge—that means the Red Mill—Moulin—Desmoulins—Pierre Desmoulins was Peter of the Mills.

"That's it!" Nancy suddenly cried. "Pierre Desmoulins is Peter Mills. It's the same name!"

Frank's expression was blank.

"Peter Mills was one of the people I said Danielle might have been visiting at that hotel in the Latin Quarter," Nancy said. "I think I know where Jack is being held. We'd better call Inspector Bertholet right away."

She started in the direction of the doorway, but Joe stopped her.

"I'll go," he said. "You stay here and make the drop. It's almost midnight now."

As Joe disappeared through the ballroom door, Nancy looked at the big clock on the wall by the bandstand. Just one minute to midnight. People around the room began counting down the seconds to the New Year.

Nancy edged through the crowd to the largest Christmas tree. It had about a dozen packages at its base, but none with purple paper or a pink ribbon.

She listened to the count, then took the package from her shopping bag and set it on the floor exactly at midnight. An instant later every light in the room went out.

"Happy New Year!" people shouted. Someone let out a shriek, and another voice called, "Keep calm. Someone's gone to turn the power back on."

When at last the lights came back on, Nancy looked down—and her heart turned over.

The package was gone!

Chapter Nineteen

FRANK!" NANCY EXCLAIMED. "Pierre and Danielle got away with the package while the lights were off!"

"They can't have gotten far," he told her. "Let's go."

As they raced across the room, Nancy kept scanning the crowd, but she saw neither of them.

They ran into Joe on their way out of the ballroom. "It's all set, you guys—" he began. "Hey, what's going on?" he asked as Frank yanked on his arm.

"There's been a change of plans, Joe," Frank told him. "We'll talk as we go." He and Nancy quickly explained the situation while the three of them made their way to the hotel lobby.

Nancy paused to catch her breath as they entered the lobby, her eyes taking in every detail. Suddenly she caught sight of a fringed cowgirl's jacket, just disappearing out the hotel entrance.

"Over there!" she said hoarsely. "Quick!"

She broke into a run, dodging around surprised hotel guests and bursting out into the cold night air. Twenty yards away Danielle was walking in her cowgirl outfit next to a masked man dressed as the Phantom of the Opera. The man had the purple and pink package in his hand.

So *that* was Pierre's costume, she thought, starting after them.

"Nancy, wait," Frank cautioned in a whisper. "If they see us, we won't have a chance. We've got to surprise them.

"If we can stay hidden on the other side of those cars, we may be able to catch up to them without their noticing."

Moving as silently as possible, they slipped across the street and ducked down on the street side of the row of cars. They ran in the same direction as the couple. Luckily, it was late and there was no traffic on the road.

Nancy risked a glance through a car window

moments later. Pierre and Danielle were only a few yards ahead.

Frank motioned for Joe and Nancy to cut around and surprise the crooks, while he stayed behind to block their retreat.

Nancy's heart was pounding as she and Joe made one final sprint, then burst out from between two cars, right in front of Pierre and Danielle.

"Hold it!" Joe shouted.

Pierre flung his cape back over his shoulder and drew the revolver from Danielle's holster. He pointed it straight at Joe.

"If you try to stop me, you're dead," Pierre said in a voice that left no doubt as to his seriousness.

"You can't get away with this," Nancy said, trying not to look at the gun. "We know you're holding Jack at your room at the Auberge des Remparts. The police are already on their way there."

Danielle's mouth dropped open. "How did you know—" she began.

"Do not say a word!" he growled, then muttered something in French. He glared at Nancy and Joe with such evil intensity that Nancy felt the hairs rise on the back of her neck.

"It does not matter what you know," Pierre snarled. "Danielle and I will be far from here by the time your inspector friend finds your bodies." He raised the shiny gun and aimed.

At the same instant, Frank appeared behind Pierre and Danielle. Before the couple could even turn around, Frank had launched a powerful karate kick that knocked the revolver from Pierre's hand. As Frank fell to the concrete he caught himself on his palms and brought his legs around to sweep Pierre off his feet. An instant later Joe pounced on Pierre, kneeling on his chest. Frank pinned his arms down.

The purple package had gone flying from Pierre's grasp. As Nancy turned to get it, she saw that Danielle had already snatched it from the ground and was running down the sidewalk.

"Not a chance," Nancy muttered, sprinting after Danielle. She leapt forward in a flying tackle that left Danielle stretched out on the pavement.

As Nancy pinned the petite race car driver's arms behind her back, she heard sirens approaching. The noise became deafening as three police cars tore down the street toward them, lights flashing. They screeched to a halt, and moments later Nancy, Frank, Joe, Pierre, and Danielle were surrounded by uniformed officers.

"Ah, Mademoiselle Drew and the Hardys,"

Inspector Bertholet said, pushing through the circle. "I hope you have had an exciting New Year's Eve?"

Joe made a wry smile. "That's for sure," he said.

The inspector waved a hand at Pierre and Danielle. "My men can take care of these two," he said, "but I believe we still need to free your friend. Shall we go to this Auberge des Remparts you were telling me about?"

Nancy, Frank, and Joe grinned at one another. "What are we waiting for?" said Nancy.

"This party was a really good idea, Frank," Nancy said the next afternoon.

"Henri insisted," Frank told her. "He said after all we've been through, we deserve a celebration."

Nancy helped herself to some punch from the buffet table in Henri Dussault's dining room, then placed a small sandwich and a miniature cream puff on her plate. "It's great to see Emily looking so happy," she said. "I don't think she's ever going to let Jack out of her sight again."

She gestured through a curved archway to where Emily and Jack were snuggled close together on a love seat. Bess, Dennis, Joe, and Mike Adams were all nearby, seated on chairs or lounging on the plush carpeting. At the other end of the room, near the fireplace, Henri and François Volnay were talking in low voices.

"That night, after I left you guys, I went to Mike's place and developed the film I'd shot that day," Jack was saying as Nancy and Frank joined them. "The shots from the Auto Federation publicity shoot came out really well, so I enlarged the best shots and early the next morning I made an appointment with the big enchilada at the Federation."

He frowned, adding, "I had no idea Pierre was a total creep."

"None of us did," said Joe, swallowing a tiny turkey sandwich in one bite and reaching for another.

"It was just by chance that the location at the Notre Dame Basilica was on the way to the Federation," Jack explained. "I figured I would drop off my camera bag in the production trailer so I wouldn't have to lug it around."

"Boy, am I glad you did," Emily told him. "Otherwise, who knows what Pierre would have done to you."

In response, Jack wrapped his arm more firmly around Emily's shoulders. "Anyway," he went on, "Pierre seemed impressed when I showed him my eight-by-tens. I figured I had the gig for sure. Then he went to get something from another office. The next thing I knew, I was in that hotel room, tied to the bed, with a headache that would be ten on the Richter scale."

He let out a long breath. "Pierre and that girl, Danielle, kept me tied and gagged the whole time except for when they gave me stuff to eat."

"It must have been awful," said Bess, leaning back against an oversize pillow.

"All's well that ends well," Jack said with a shrug. "I'm just glad Pierre and Danielle are behind bars."

Frank nodded his agreement. "Inspector Bertholet told us that when his men showed Pierre and Danielle the photograph of Pierre planting the bomb in Junot's car, they finally cracked and admitted everything," he said. "Apparently, Junot overheard Pierre and Danielle talking about their plans to steal the prize fund, and he began blackmailing them. We were right about those two-thousand-dollar withdrawals being hush money, by the way. The bank finally traced the account the money was transferred to. It was in Junot's name, not Pierre's."

"Of course," Nancy put in. "Junot was the one getting the payoff, after all. And that way Pierre knew the transaction still couldn't be traced directly to him."

"Pierre also admitted to hiring two mechanics as goons," said Joe, picking up where his brother left off. "They were the masked guys who went after Nancy on the Promenade des Gouverneurs, and who ransacked the photography studio and beat up Mike."

Mike rubbed the bruise that still darkened his forehead above one eye. "I won't forget those guys for a long time," he said.

"We were right about the note, too," Nancy added. "Inspector Bertholet's men traced it to the typewriter in Pierre's office at the Auto Federation's temporary headquarters."

"There's one thing I don't get," said Mike. "I mean, it seems as if Pierre was the brains behind this operation. What was in it for Danielle?"

Joe turned to Mike and said, "You mean besides a big cut of the money? According to Inspector Bertholet, Pierre promised to give Danielle lots of exposure within the Auto Federation and in the racing circuit." He made a wry smile. "You had her pegged right the first time you saw her, Bess. I mean, she was willing to actually kill someone in order to get ahead."

"Not to mention kidnap Jack," Bess added. She gazed thoughtfully at the pâté on her plate for a moment, then said, "It's funny. I mean, we were so convinced that Jack had been taken by the person who was sabotaging *Dangerous*

Loves. But Grant didn't have anything to do with it."

Joe nodded. "So as a result of our cases, the Auto Federation doesn't have a director anymore, and *Dangerous Loves* doesn't have an assistant director," he said.

"I wouldn't worry about *Dangerous Loves,*" Jack put in, smiling proudly at Emily. "David has already found the perfect replacement for Grant Shulman."

Emily's cheeks turned pink. "I hope I can do a good job—" she began.

"Are you kidding?" Bess exclaimed, jumping up to hug her cousin. "You'll be great! Congratulations, Em. You really deserve it."

Glancing back to where Dennis was sitting in an upholstered chair, she said, "Actually, Dennis has some good news, too."

The actor leaned forward and said, "I got a call from my agent just before coming over here. You remember that Hollywood feature movie that I was offered a part in? Well, it won't be going into production for a few weeks yet, which means I can finish shooting *Dangerous Loves* and still take the new part."

"That *is* good news," Nancy agreed. She popped the miniature cream puff into her mouth, then licked the chocolate off her fingers. She looked up as Henri Dussault and François Volnay came over to join them.

"While you are all making announcements, I have one also that I would like to make," Henri said. He clapped François around the shoulders, giving him a warm smile. "Permit me to present the new director of the Quebec Auto Federation—François Volnay."

As everyone cheered, Nancy leaned back contentedly. "Well, you guys, last year sure went out with a bang," she said as the room quieted again. "But I have a feeling this year we'll all have lots to celebrate."

She raised her glass of punch, and everyone else followed suit. "Happy New Year, everyone!"